I0534393

Ciaran

Ciaran

A BOURBON & BLOOD NOVELLA

CHASITY BOWLIN

Ciaran
Paperback Edition
Copyright © 2025 by Chasity Bowlin

Love N. Books Press
An Imprint of Wolfpack Publishing
1707 E. Diana Street
Tampa, FL 33610

www.lovenbookspress.com

All rights reserved. No part of this book may be reproduced in any form or by any electronic or mechanical means, including information storage and retrieval systems, without express written permission from the publisher, except for the use of brief quotations in reviews. Any use of this publication to train generative artificial intelligence (AI) technologies is expressly prohibited.

This book is a work of fiction. References to historical events, real people, or real places are used fictitiously. Any similarity to real persons, living or dead, is purely coincidental and not intended by the author.

All brand names and product names used in this book are trademarks, registered trademarks, or trade names of their respective holders. Wolfpack Publishing is not associated with any product or vendor in this book.

Cover design by Jennilynn Wyer Designs
Edited by My Brother's Editor

Ciaran was originally self-published in 2024 by Chasity Bowlin.

Paperback ISBN 979-8-89567-984-5
Ebook ISBN 979-8-89567-983-8
LCCN 2025933076

Ciaran

Prologue

Neon lights advertising check cashing, female dancers, and adult novelties winked from the dirty windows of the rundown buildings that lined the street. The unmarked police vehicle pulled up outside the dingy bar off Winchester Road, and people scattered like cockroaches. Even without the flashing lights and logo, the vehicle's origins were obvious. The blacked-out windows and flashing neon panties that adorned the building gave little doubt as to what sort of establishment it was and the fact that the car clearly did not belong. Lexington, Kentucky, wasn't the biggest city, but it had its fair share of crime, most of it drug-related.

He did not want to be there. It was too risky, too damned dirty, and too close for comfort. If someone saw him, he was screwed. Cops, even dirty ones, had images to uphold. Getting out of the car, he approached the door and the sketchy doorman. "I need to see Sergei."

"Ten dollars," the doorman replied, his thick Russian accent difficult to decipher.

Grabbing the man by the jacket, he hauled him up

until they were nose to nose. "Do I look stupid to you? Walk in and get caught on camera? Not fucking likely, genius. Get Sergei out here or, so help me God, I'll knock every goddamn rotten tooth out of your head."

He released the man abruptly, sending him sprawling onto the pavement. Without a backward glance, he headed to the small alley between the club and the seedy auto service next door. At the very least, he wouldn't be out in the open where any asshole could recognize him. Reaching into his jacket pocket, he produced a pack of cigarettes and lit one of them. He took a deep draw and then coughed. The things were killing him, but something had to.

After several minutes had passed, the back door of the bar opened, and a tall, thin man emerged in the alley and walked toward him. "You're not supposed to be here," he said, his accent still thick but less pronounced than the doorman's.

"We've got problems," he replied. "Crawford busted your mule, and he sang like a damn bird."

Sergei shrugged. "He's unimportant."

The cop rolled his eyes. "He was until he sold out Grigori. Yeah. That fucker is in custody now, and your supply chain went to shit...not to mention the obvious fact that Grigori is connected to me. They dig too much on this, and we all go to hell. Clearing it up any for you?"

The man uttered a curse in Russian. "Does he know about you? If he does, it's too late. We're fucked."

"Not yet, but if we don't do something, he will soon enough."

"How do you suggest we distract him?"

The cop leaned back against the block wall of the building. "There's only one thing that asshole cares about more than he cares about being a cop...that's his bitch of a sister."

The Russian chuckled. "She turned you down?"

She had, but that was beside the point. "Whatever it takes. We need to divert his attention. Handle her. She's the distraction we need!"

"Define handle," Sergei demanded.

"Use your fucking imagination! This ain't kindergarten, and I'm not holding your goddamn hand! Jesus, even the fucking criminals lack initiative these days!" He punctuated his diatribe by tossing his cigarette to the ground and crushing it under the heel of his shoe.

Sergei shook his head. "You want me to kidnap her? Where the hell am I supposed to hide a cop's sister? Here? You're crazy."

"I never said kidnapping or killing. That stays on the back burner for now. Just hurt her enough to distract him and to let him know she's not safe as long as he keeps playing boy-scout."

"You want her shot, stabbed, beaten, raped? You wanted to be the boss here, be the fucking boss and issue an order," Sergei snapped. "*Chertovski mudak!*"

"Call me a fucking asshole again, and I'll rip your damn throat out," he said. "Yeah. I might not speak Russian, but I been around you fuckers enough to have picked up a few words. I didn't say how, Sergei, and I don't fucking care. Make it happen, or we all go down together."

He didn't wait for the Russian's answer but walked away, back to his unmarked car. He had an alibi to establish.

One

Loralei Crawford sighed wearily as she turned off the lights in her small and on-the-verge-of-failing boutique. Expensive and exclusive, she'd opened at the right time to hit all the traffic of people coming into town for the equestrian games. She'd gotten too cocky during the boom phase, and now she was dealing with the bust.

A heavy sigh escaped her and filled the small space. It was eight o'clock on the dot, and all she wanted was to get home to her dog and a DVR-ed episode of *The Walking Dead*. She could lust over Daryl's arms and forget about the real world for a bit.

It had been a long, slow day, and other than a few online inquiries, she'd sold not a single thing. The situation wasn't dire yet. She'd done well enough during derby and prom season to get through the lean, late summer months. Fall and winter would be slower still, with the possible exception of a boost around New Year's Eve and Valentine's Day. Then two more brutal months until prom season started again.

To say the very least, it was an eye-opener about the pitfalls of owning one's own business. She'd spent the day scrolling through Facebook and playing Candy Crush. If she were honest with herself, she'd admit it wasn't the slow sales that had her down. It was him. Two months since she'd seen him or heard from him. No calls, no texts. It was like he'd just dropped off the face of the planet. It pissed her off that she couldn't get him out of her head, even though she'd told herself a hundred times it was for the best. She'd never really believed it would work out. He'd been too charming, too sexy, and just too much. Ciaran Darcy was the perfect man to have an affair with, but not a relationship.

It might have been two months since she'd even laid eyes on him, but she was no closer to getting over him than she had been the day he just walked out. Their relationship hadn't been a particularly long one, but the three months they'd been together had been enough for her to know that he was *The One*. He made her feel like no one else ever had, but it had apparently been one-sided. He'd left without a backward glance.

Disheartened, Loralei wanted nothing more than to get home, put on a pair of yoga pants, and dive headfirst into a tub of Graeter's mint chocolate chip ice cream. It wouldn't improve the situation, but it would do a hell of a lot for her mood. Since she could do all of that while cuddling her behaviorally challenged pug, Churchill, it would be a win for them both.

Backing through the door, juggling bags and keys, Loralei didn't see the man who emerged from the white van parked in the alley. It wasn't until she felt the force of the blow at her shoulder, a blow that sent her stumbling back into the shop to sprawl on the floor, that she even realized something was wrong.

Rolling onto her back, stunned and disoriented, Loralei looked up at the strange man who had forced his way into the shop. His long blond hair was pulled back into a ponytail, and he had intricate tattoos on his neck, though she couldn't see what they were under his collar.

Details. She took in the leather jacket he wore, the rings and chains, the exaggerated bone structure. All this was running through her mind, her brother, Matt's, lessons and lectures about being a good witness drilled into her over the years, as she scrambled backward.

Her hand landed on the key ring she'd dropped a moment earlier. Keys wouldn't be the most effective weapon, but at least they were something. Gripping them, allowing the sharp points to protrude between her fingers, she knew she would only have one opportunity, and it would have to count. When her back pressed up against the counter, she braced herself for what was coming.

The man stood over her and pulled a wicked-looking knife from his belt. "I have a message for your brother." He had a thick accent from somewhere in Eastern Europe, though she'd never be able to narrow it down beyond that.

Loralei clutched the keys tighter, feeling them dig into her own hand. "Well, he isn't here, asshole!"

"It is okay. You will be the message," the man said with a chuckle. The sound was terrifying. It might have been about "business," but it was clear to her then that he enjoyed his work.

He was on her in an instant, but Loralei hadn't grown up on a horse farm, wrestling with her brother and his best friend, Grant, for nothing. She brought her knees up, catching him in the gut and sending the first pass of the blade wide. It sliced into her shoulder, the burning pain

7

exploding when he pulled it free. With her empty hand, Loralei reached up, clawing at his eyes.

Even when his fist connected again, slamming into her, she didn't give up. Temporarily blinded by her fingernails, he didn't see the keys clutched in her other hand until they connected with his face. Blood spewed from his nose, and one of the keys had split his lip. His fist slammed into her face, and stars exploded before her eyes. Darkness threatened, hovering around the edges of her vision.

She fought against it, struggling to hold on to consciousness just as she struggled against him. He wasn't very big, but he was strong. Still, they were the same height, and she probably outweighed him by a good fifty pounds. Manhandling her wasn't the easiest thing for him to do. Somehow, Loralei managed to put a few feet between them. He lunged with the knife, the blade glancing off her ankle bone as Loralei tumbled into a display of necklaces.

The cement replica of the *Venus de Milo* that she used to display jewelry tumbled to the ground. It was small but weighed around ten pounds. She hadn't set the alarm yet, but the windows were wired to trigger it automatically if the glass was broken. Reaching for the statue, Loralei threw it with all her might, sending it crashing into the nearest window. The glass broke, and when it did, the sound of the alarm rang out through the shop. The phone began to ring immediately, the security company calling to verify the situation.

"Fat fucking bitch!" he screamed at her. The knife came down again, but she managed to roll away so that it only glanced off her thigh.

Loralei grabbed at the debris that littered the floor and threw whatever she could get her hands on at him. The necklaces and display stands weren't the most effective weapons, but they slowed him down. After a few seconds, when the first wail of sirens sounded in the distance, he cursed again and made for the door.

Bleeding, hurting, trembling with adrenaline and fear, Loralei lay there, waiting for him to return, waiting for him to come back and finish her off. She was still waiting for him when the flashing blue lights from the patrol cars spilled through the broken window and the first uniformed officer entered through the door. Only then did she give in to the tears.

It always surprises me how much all barns smell the same."

Ciaran Darcy looked up from the tack he was cleaning and cursed. His Irish brogue was heavy with exhaustion and the whiskey that had been his companion for the better part of the evening. To see Grant Ashworth walking in as if he already owned the place, lock, stock, and barrel, had him spoiling for a fight.

The two of them were neighbors, but that was all they had in common. Grant was part of the same silver spoon set that Loralei had been born into, and it rubbed him a little raw. Sure, Grant had always treated her like a little sister, and Loralei's affection for the other man could only ever have been described as familial, but it had still bugged the hell out of him because he'd felt excluded. *Whose fault was that, you shite?*

The all-too-honest voice in his head only pissed Ciaran off more, so he turned the full force of his shitty mood on the man who'd just intruded. "Get the fuck out of my barn. You don't own it yet, you right bastard!"

Grant pulled his hands from his pockets and left them clenched at his sides. With his feet spread wide and his jaw clenched, it was clear Ciaran wasn't the only one looking to burn off some steam. "I'll go when I'm 'fooking' ready."

"You've a piss-poor imitation of an Irishman," Ciaran declared and rose to his feet. With his hands planted on his lean hips, he faced off with the other man. Grant outweighed him by a stone and had at least two inches on him in height, but both of them knew, if it came to blows, Ciaran would walk away the winner. "Say what you want and get out."

Grant clearly hadn't anticipated the invitation. He rocked back on his heels and shook his head. "I want to hire you."

"It'll be a cold day in hell. I'll not take a pittance from you to run a farm that's my own." Ciaran bit the words out angrily. He was struggling to keep it afloat, fighting off foreclosure with tooth and claw. Grant wanted the land because it was adjacent to his. If their situations were reversed, Ciaran knew he'd want the same, but it didn't make it any easier to swallow. The mix of anger and whiskey that burned in his gut was heady, and he could feel his control as it started to slip.

Grant shook his head. "You'll never let a man speak, will you? Always rushing to conclusions and assuming the world is out to get you! I've come here to make you an offer, Darcy...and if you'd shut your damn mouth long enough to listen to it, you'd realize that it just might save your ass!"

"Then get on with it!" Ciaran demanded.

"It's security."

Ciaran shook his head, a knee-jerk reaction. "I don't do that anymore."

Grant leveled an assessing stare at him. "Even for Loralei?"

The name was like a punch in the gut. "What does she need with security?" He couldn't quite bring himself to say her name. That scar was a little too fresh to be picked at.

Grant eyed the bottle of whiskey. "The story'd be a little easier to tell if you were inclined to share some of that."

"I only drink with friends," Ciaran replied sharply. "But if it will shrink the distance between you and the point you're rambling on to, help yourself."

Grant stepped forward and picked up the bottle. A glance at the label would tell anyone that it wasn't sipping whiskey. He tipped the bottle back and took a healthy swallow before he came up coughing. "God above! I'd rather drink gasoline."

"Not all of us can afford your rarefied spirits," Ciaran said, dark amusement tinting his voice. He enjoyed watching Grant squirm. It was nice to get a little of his own back. "If you want to make an offer, you best make it before I run out of patience."

"I'll pay the mortgage on this farm, and you can use Genghis for stud for one year...if you look after Loralei."

That was a hell of an offer. It was so good in fact that Ciaran knew instantly something was very wrong. "What the hell has she gotten herself into?"

Grant took another long draw from the whiskey bottle. "It isn't what she got into. Matt made a drug bust, and it's gone sideways. They want to teach him a lesson, and they're willing to use her to do it."

Ciaran grabbed the bottle and took a swig. "You're gonna have to run that by me one more time."

Grant moved toward a hay bale and eased himself down onto it. He shook his head as if to clear it. "Jesus! That stuff will rot your brain before it rots your gut!"

"Get on with it, Ashworth!" Ciaran said. "Where is Loralei, and is she safe right now?"

Grant nodded. "She's at UK. Bastard cut her up a bit, but it's not serious. They were more worried about the knock on the head when she fell and about how clean the damned knife was."

Ciaran sat down on the hay bale facing him. "The fucker is dead. I get my hands on him, and he's a goddamn corpse. You tell her asshole brother that, will you? He can arrest me if he likes."

"I think he'd be more inclined to thank you for it. She gave the cops a description of him. They're on the lookout."

"And they'll expect her to testify in court against him, no doubt. Let's just paint a fucking target on her while we're at it!" Cold fury bubbled inside Ciaran. Loralei was too good for her own good. The police asked for a description, and she provided one because that's what good citizens did. Never once did any of those bastards tell her that speaking out against a drug dealer's hitman was as good as signing her own death warrant. "Why didn't Matt stop her?"

Grant shook his head, clearly befuddled by just how fucked up the day had become. "He didn't know. The dispatcher was new, and when the call came through from the security company, it was routed to someone else. It wasn't until one of the patrolmen recognized her that anyone even called him."

Ciaran shook his head. "Someone will get their arse handed to them over that."

Grant nodded. "You have the skills, Ciaran. I love her like my own sister, and there's no one better qualified to keep her safe...even if you are the last person she'd want to lay eyes on."

Ciaran hung his head, and a heavy sigh escaped him. "For the record, I'm not doing this for the farm. Whatever happens, the two have nothing to do with one another... now, drive me to the damn hospital. I'm too drunk for it."

Two

Loralei opened her eyes through the haze of pain medication. Something felt very wrong. With her arm in a sling and a heavy bandage on her forehead, she struggled to recall everything that had happened. When the memories did come, it wasn't in a trickle but a flood. Disjointed images of an angry man, the gleaming arc of the knife as glass shattered around them. Everything was there but jumbled and out of sync.

Reaching out, she grasped the bedrail, attempted to pull herself up. She had no destination, no notion of where she was going. But panic had her in its grip, and she could only think of one thing—run.

The machine beside her beeped as the sensor pulled loose from her fingers. The IV line tangled between her fingers. She felt trapped, and the breath caught in her lungs.

"Settle down, *milish*. You're safe here."

The soft brogue could only belong to one man. Even in her present state, it cut through the panic, through the violence and ugliness of her day. It stilled everything inside her but the beating of her heart. Even that was different when he was present. "What are you doing here, Ciaran?"

He leaned forward from the shadowy corner where he perched. "I'm here to watch over you while you sleep."

She snorted then. "You're no guardian angel."

"Even Lucifer had wings once upon a time. Sleep, love. You've nothing to fear."

Except for you. She didn't say it, but it hovered on the tip of her tongue. Ciaran would never harm her physically, but there was no one on earth who could do more damage to her emotionally. "You should go. I'd rather take my chances."

"It's not really up to you. I'll be watching over you, whether I do it from in here, out in the hallway, or with a rifle and a scope from the parking garage across the street. You're in over your head, *mavourneen.*"

"I always am with you," she said. Her eyes had adjusted enough that she could see him clearly. His jaw was dark with several days' growth of beard, and his curly hair that never seemed to tame for more than a minute at a time was wild and disheveled. He had dirt on his clothes, and she was pretty sure she could smell the whiskey on him. "You look like hell."

"You'll turn my head with such sweet talk," he said with a quick grin.

God, that grin hurt her to her soul. As her aunt would have said, that man could have sold coal to the devil. Charming, too handsome for his own good, and with just enough darkness in him to set every good girl's heart beating a bit faster, he lured her, seduced her, made her yearn for things that could never be, and he could do it all without even a touch.

He rose and moved toward the bed, coming to stand over her. Loralei looked up at him and felt herself slipping, falling back into the same desperation that had plagued her during the few short months when she'd thought he might possibly love her back. His hand closed over hers, gently guiding it toward him.

"What are you doing?" she asked.

With his other hand, he pressed the call button on her bedrail. "Making sure you can't cancel the request. You need pain medication...and possibly a sedative."

"I do not!"

He shook his head. "You've white lines around your mouth, a sure sign you're hurting. And I can smell your fear, Loralei. Tomorrow is soon enough to face it all. Trust me on that."

"I can't trust you on anything!" she snapped. "Just leave. Please!"

"I can't. I won't. I made a promise," he said.

"Like those mean so much to you."

"I never promised you anything, Loralei. Not once. Maybe I should have."

He was right. She knew that. It was her own foolish hopes and expectations that had broken her heart. "If I take the drugs from the nurse, will you go?"

"No. But you won't even know I'm here. So take them anyway and escape it all for a bit...even me."

It didn't matter anyway. He was on her mind all the time whether he was present or not. Her friends had pressured her into dating again because she'd become a hermit since things had gone south with Ciaran. It clearly had not gone as planned. Now he was not only on her mind but back in her life, and there wasn't a hope in hell she'd come out of it unscathed, even if he did manage to save her life. "I'll know," she said softly.

The nurse entered then, a hypodermic needle in her hand. She fiddled with the IV a bit, but before she'd even finished, Loralei felt the wave take her. Her vision blurred, and the last thing she saw before the blackness claimed her again was Ciaran's face.

Ciaran watched her sleep, the pain medication having eased some of the tension from her face. She looked like hell. A dark and ugly bruise had taken shape on the crest of her cheekbone. He'd taken enough punches to know that the bastard had landed one or two on her. Her hands were torn up, scraped and bloody. He knew from the nurse that she had three knife wounds, one in her shoulder that was serious enough to require monitoring and two minor wounds at her ankle and thigh respectively.

Everything he saw told him one thing and one thing alone. She'd fought like a demon when the bastard cornered her. He might have gotten in a few good licks, but he was fairly certain Loralei had gotten in a few of her own. That appeased him somewhat. It wouldn't stop him from gutting the bastard, but it helped.

He couldn't take his eyes off her. Even banged up, bruised, and bloodied, she was perfect to him. Just looking at her was like a punch in the gut. He leaned forward and, with only one finger, gently traced one of the scrapes that ran from her wrist up her arm, nearly to her elbow. It wasn't right that she had to fight so hard. It wasn't right that he hadn't been there to protect her.

That thought had come unbidden to his mind. He'd been running since the day he walked out of her house. Even before then, he'd been revving the engine and looking for an exit.

It wasn't just that he didn't want a relationship. It wasn't even that he was terrified of commitment, though that was probably true. The intensity of what he felt for her had rocked him to the core and left him shaking like a scared boy. She made him yearn for things a man like him shouldn't want, and she'd given him just enough hope to make it utterly terrifying. So, he'd picked a fight. He'd behaved like a jealous prick, and then he'd walked out on her because it was better, he'd reasoned, to at least have it end on his terms rather than have her reject him when she finally figured out what he was really worth.

He'd made a mess of it all. A dozen times—hell, a hundred times—he'd picked up the phone to call her, to try to explain. Every time, he'd hung it up before even letting it ring. That ugly voice inside his head would rear up and tell him all the ways he wasn't good enough, all the ways she deserved better. Looking at her, he realized he didn't care. No one else would love her as well or fight for her as hard, and no one else would protect her the way he would. He'd just have to convince her of it.

The door opened, but he didn't bother to get up. He knew who it was.

"What the fuck are you doing in here?"

Ciaran didn't take umbrage at the rude tone. Matt had a right to be suspicious. He was Loralei's brother, after all, and being confronted with the sight of the man who'd broken his sister's heart, or at the very least, taken a healthy chunk out of her pride, was enough to put any man on edge. "I'm looking after her...or didn't Grant bloody Ashworth share that bit of info with you?"

"He did," Matt agreed, depositing a takeout bag and his laptop on the bedside table. Empty handed, he turned to glare at Ciaran. "I just didn't expect you to be hovering over her like some tragic hero...which you're not, by the way. Neither tragic nor heroic."

Ciaran grinned. "I never claimed to be either."

Matt shrugged out of his jacket, and his tie followed. "What about a lying asshole? Did you ever claim to be that? You might have a case there."

"I never lied to her," Ciaran said. "I won't deny being an asshole, but I never lied."

Matt studied him for a moment. "So what happens now? You come in, play the hero, fuck with her head again, and then you're out the door?"

Ciaran looked up at the other man but didn't answer immediately. He paused long enough that the silence grew taut and uncomfortable before stating emphatically, "That's not a discussion I mean to have with you. Any discussions about what's to happen between Loralei and myself will take place between Loralei and myself. You're entitled to have any opinion on it if you wish, but you're not entitled to participate."

Matt shook his head. "Get out. I've got her for tonight, and maybe by tomorrow I won't feel quite as shitty about sticking her with you. But I warn you, Darcy, you hurt her again, you bring one more tear to her eye, and I swear to God, I will end you."

"You're welcome to try," Ciaran said easily as he rose from the hard plastic chair and headed for the door. He'd come back the following day when Loralei was released. It'd be best to get rested up and prepared for whatever might be coming their way.

"You're an asshole," Matt said.

"Yes. I am," Ciaran agreed as the door closed softly behind him.

The following afternoon, Loralei sat perched on the edge of her hospital bed, dressed in black leggings and a flowing tunic. In deference to her stitches, bandages, and the fact that she felt like she'd been hit by a truck, her fashionista status had been forfeited for the time being.

Kaitlyn, Grant's gorgeous wife who had somehow taken on the role of her best friend when no one was looking, had done her makeup, which meant she was wearing far more of the stuff than she was comfortable with, though to be fair, she looked like she'd thrown a fight and probably needed it. Since Kaitlyn's go-to method of dealing with long hair was to simply whack it all off, Loralei had eschewed her assistance there. With a great deal of difficulty, she'd managed to pull it back into a low messy bun. It was a look, overall, but not necessarily a good one. Of course, she reasoned, she'd been stabbed and beaten. She was entitled to look like hell.

Matt paced the length of her hospital room as they waited for the doctor to come and discharge her. "You have to, Loralei," he finally said. "I don't like it either, but it's the best option."

"The hell I do," Loralei responded sharply. "I'm not bringing him into my house!"

"No," Matt agreed. "You're not. Your house is too difficult to secure. Small backyard with lots of bushes and shrubs for people to hide in, too many windows and doors to be effectively secured. It's a goddamn logistical nightmare."

Loralei would have rolled her eyes, but her head already hurt badly enough without fueling that fire.

Instead, she leveled a baleful stare at him. "Stop being so damned literal. You know what I meant!"

Matt stared back at her, unflinching. There was no give in him, no softness. This wasn't one of those times when she could bat her eyelashes and soften up her big brother.

"You'll go to the farm with Darcy," he said firmly. "And for the record, I don't like it, and I don't like him. But I looked at his service history, Lor, or at least the part of it that I could see. He's got skills you need."

Ciaran had a lot of skills, and most of them meant trouble for her. Of course, that was the last thing Matt would want to hear from her. But she knew about Ciaran's service record or at least had some vague notion. He had never been especially forthcoming about his background, but he had told her he spent almost a decade in the Irish Special Forces.

Memories of their first meeting in the darkened dive bar just a mile from Grant and Kaitlyn's home swept through her. The brawl had broken out near the pool tables but had soon swept up every patron. Some man three times his size had sent Ciaran tumbling halfway across the barroom where he'd landed face down in her lap. He'd gotten up with a cheeky grin and a filthy comment and had jumped right back into the fray. When it was all over and done, he'd bought her a drink, put her in a taxi, and somehow charmed her phone number from her. His aim had clearly been more than a phone number, but he'd settled for that graciously enough.

She'd like to blame it on the whiskey she'd been drinking that night, but the simple fact of the matter was, she would probably have given it to him anyway. Ciaran was beautiful in the way that only Black Irish could be. With his charming accent, perfect smile, and his body which was utter perfection, it would have taken a stronger woman than her to resist him.

"It doesn't matter. You're all overreacting to this anyway. The attacker won't come back," she insisted. Even to her own ears, it rang false, but it was the version of the story she preferred.

Matt glanced at her, his expression firm. The worry and stress had left its mark on him. Matt had been blessed with a baby face, but for the first time in their lives, he looked older than his years. "Don't be stupid. We both know that's not the case. Men like this don't just go away. He's former Russian Mafia, for fuck's sake! If he's been ordered to see you dead, he will kill you or will die trying."

"He said he had a message to deliver. It's delivered. It's done!"

"The hell it is!" Matt shouted. "They did this to you to get to me...as long as I'm working this case, they know you're my weakness. I can't do my job and protect you! And in case you didn't stop to think about it, let me sum it up for you. These fuckers are cruel...vicious, brutal, and colder than anything you can imagine. There are things worse than dying, Loralei, and they'll put you through every damn one of them!"

That scared her. Terrified her actually. Matt was always one to gloss over details and tell her things would be fine. The fact that he actually wanted her to be fearful was a new and truly terrifying experience. "Fine. But does it have to be him? Can't you put me in protective custody in a safe house with a couple of cute, uniformed officers at the door?"

He didn't bat an eye. "There's no money in the budget for a protective detail for you. For once in your damn life, just listen to me and let me keep you safe."

"This is Lexington! We don't have Russian Mafia!"

Matt sat down in the same ugly chair Ciaran had occupied for most of the night. "No. We've got the assholes they didn't want...a bunch of fucking Mafia rejects who would rather shoot you, stab you, and rape you—and quite possibly in that order—than look at you. This is big, Loralei, and if I don't stop it now, this city is going straight to hell."

"What is this really about, Matt?" she demanded.

"You've heard of Krokodile?"

"It's a drug, but I didn't think we had it here," she answered.

"We do now. Drug dealers are ambitious, Lor, and they're always looking for new territory. I busted one two days ago, and not small time, either. He was carrying enough of this to supply the city for a month. He's also selling out his friends like it's a damn auction. Good for me, but bad for you. Less than twenty-four hours later, one of them was at your door. They want to make an example of me. This, everything that happened to you, is my damn fault."

She could see how worried he was, and she could see the guilt that was eating at him over it. "It isn't your fault."

"When I booked this guy, he told me they'd be coming after mine, and I just blew it off," Matt added. "Please, Loralei, I have to nail these guys, and I can't do that until I know that you're safe."

She shook her head. "I don't like it. I don't want him back in my life, Matt. I was finally getting over it...over him. I can't do this again." It humbled her to admit it, made her feel weak and needy.

"I know he hurt you...and he's not a long-haul kinda guy. But right now, if I have to choose between having you alive and brokenhearted or tortured and killed because of me, it's a damned easy choice," Matt stated. "Besides, he's on his way here now."

Loralei rolled her eyes heavenward. "So asking me if I'd be willing to let Ciaran look after me was really just to humor me? Once again, my life choices were made via royal Crawford decree!"

Matt ran his hand over his face in an expression of frustration. "It's not like that...this isn't Mom monitoring your calories and bitching about your weight! You are the only family I have, or at least the only family I claim. If keeping you safe means stepping on your toes a little, well tough shit."

"I can come back after you've resolved your family crisis." The charm of the Irish accent was overshadowed by sarcasm.

Loralei looked up to see Ciaran standing in the doorway, holding a pet carrier that rattled with familiar snores. Her heart melted a little at the sight of Churchill and at the sight of the man carrying her precious, and somewhat challenged, pug. But she had to admit Ciaran didn't look much better than Matt. He had dark circles under his eyes, he was unshaven, and his curly hair was wild. But his jeans were clean and well fitting. *Lord, did they fit well!* The white T-shirt with a plaid shirt open over it was his standard uniform, as were the battered cowboy boots on his feet.

"The truck is out front if you've been sprung," he said, depositing the pet carrier on the bed beside her. Immediately, she unzipped it and reached inside for Churchill. His squirmy little body torpedoed into her as he began his enthusiastic, happy dance all over her thighs. She winced when his paws came down on her fresh stitches. Immediately, Ciaran swooped him up. The damn traitor collapsed in his arms in a boneless and ecstatic heap, tongue lolling out and panting.

"Not yet," Matt answered for her. "Waiting on the doctor. Should be any minute."

Ciaran nodded. "You think you could give us a minute here?"

Matt narrowed his eyes at him. "That depends on what you're going to do with it."

Ciaran ducked his head, and his lips quirked upward. "I'd hardly have anything other than conversation in mind given her current condition...and her lack of inclination." He gave the dog a pat on the belly. "Besides, we're well chaperoned."

Matt huffed out a breath. "Fine. I'm going to go see if I can't move this doctor along. Why the fuck they think no one else has anything to do but wait on them I'll never know."

When Matt left, Loralei looked at Ciaran and steeled herself. "I've got nothing to say to you."

He shrugged as he absentmindedly scratched the dog's belly and set the pug's back leg to trembling furiously. "Then you can listen to what's been on my mind...I owe you an apology."

She looked away. "You don't owe me a damn thing, and even if you did, it's way too late for an I'm sorry."

He moved closer, seating himself on the edge of the bed next to her. "You can hate me forever. You're entitled. But you have to know I didn't mean to hurt you. That was always the last thing I wanted to do."

"Is that why you blow hot and cold? Because you're trying not to hurt me? It's a piss-poor strategy."

"No," he replied. "I'm not good at relationships. Never have been. I should have stayed in the damned army. I'm not fit for much else. But when I met you, I thought...no. I didn't think. I wanted, and I took, and then I ran. I was a coward, and I'm not proud of it. But, right now, there are more important things. I'll keep you safe, *mavourneen*. You might not trust me for anything else, but you can trust me for that."

"You said that last night." Her voice was soft, pitched low. When she'd woken this morning, she thought perhaps she'd dreamed the whole thing, until Matt had begun outlining his plan for her continued well-being. Just as before, Ciaran's words left her off-balance and uncertain, but then he had always been good at keeping her off balance.

"I meant it then, and I mean it now. All this, me and you, it's just until you're safe. Then everything goes back to the way it was. You'll be shed of me for good if that's what you want."

Loralei shook her head. "I don't think I can do this."

He reached out and traced one of the long scrapes that covered her hand. "I don't think you have a choice. He targeted you, love, specifically. They want your brother's focus on you and not on them. Until he's finished with this, you'll not be safe. The Russians don't fuck around. They are brutal and effective, and if they want you dead, they'll do whatever it takes to make that happen. And if they don't want you dead, they might make you wish you were. They're set to make an example of your brother, and they'll do that by going after what he cares about the most. Right now, that's you."

Loralei shuddered. She didn't want to recall just how brutal they were. It had been the element of surprise that saved her the day before. He hadn't expected her to fight back, and if he cornered her again, she wouldn't have that advantage. "Fine."

Just as she capitulated, the doctor walked in looking harried while Matt strolled in behind him looking victorious. The doctor frowned at the dog, but after a surreptitious glance at her less than pleasant-faced brother, wisely said nothing. "Well, Miss Crawford, you're free to go. The nurse is preparing your discharge instructions. You'll need to return in a week to have the stitches removed. You were very lucky."

"If I were that lucky, I wouldn't have needed stitches," she replied drolly.

The doctor's frown deepened. He clearly did not understand humor. "The nurse will be in shortly."

It was only a moment later that the nurse shuffled in with a wheelchair. "Oh, no," Loralei said. "I'm not going out in that."

The nurse shrugged. "You can go out in the chair, or you can stay here. It's up to you. Either way, that creature goes. He's drooling."

Loralei glanced over at Churchill, who, sure enough, was in fact drooling. She knew just how skilled Ciaran's hands were, and for just a moment, she was jealous of the dog.

"Get in the damn chair, Lor," Matt said. "I'm sick of this shithole."

Loralei rose from the bed and then climbed into the wheelchair. It offended her to the depths of her soul. "Fine."

"I'll get the truck," Ciaran said, handed her the dog, and walked out.

"I don't like this," Loralei said to Matt as the nurse pushed the chair down the hall. She cuddled Churchill close and tried to figure out how the hell she was going to get through this.

"I don't care."

"Asshole," she said bitterly.

"Yep."

Ciaran walked around the truck and opened the door. He didn't have to help her in. Her brother would do that, but there was no point in giving the man even more reason to despise him. It had rocked him to see Loralei in such a condition. Even with the pound of makeup Kaitlyn had slathered on her face, the bruises were glaring on her pale skin.

Her injuries, all things considered, weren't that severe. A total of twenty-seven stitches between the wound at her shoulder and the ones on her thigh and her ankle, but no one had to tell him how much worse it could have been. She'd been damned lucky to have gotten by with such minor injuries, and if she faced off against the bastard again, the outcome would be very different.

Taking the dog carrier from her, which was empty of course, as the damn dog was cuddled close to her chest, he placed it behind his seat. She loved the thing though it had less than two brain cells to rub together. It had driven him crazy the way she carried on over the little beast, but at the same time, he'd found it endearing. Her need to rescue animals and the way she melted at the sight of any baby animal had charmed him. And he'd almost lost her.

That thought kept running through his mind, but on its heels came another thought. She wasn't his. She could have been, would have been, if he hadn't been such an asshole, but he'd blown it. All that was left was to keep her safe and do his best to convince her he wasn't the worthless shite he'd behaved like.

So, he stood there like a third wheel, looking like a dumbass, as Matt helped her from the wheelchair and into the truck. When the door closed, Matt turned to him. "Your job is to make sure no one else hurts her. My job, if you hurt her again, will be to make your life hell. We clear?"

"Crystal," Ciaran replied with a nod. It goaded him, but it wasn't like he hadn't earned their distrust. Walking back around the truck, he climbed behind the wheel and met her questioning gaze. "Your brother doesn't trust me," he said.

"Should he?" she asked skeptically.

Ciaran smiled. "Probably not. Let's get you home and settled. You look like hell."

She leaned her head back against the seat and closed her eyes. "Where's that silver tongue now, Irish?"

"Ask me when you're better, and I'll demonstrate," he shot back.

"Oh, no. That's not happening. Not ever again."

We'll see, he thought, and turned the key in the ignition.

The ride to his farm wasn't a long one. They managed to avoid the worst of the day's traffic. Heading out of town toward the horse country that spanned Fayette and Woodford Counties, it was only twenty-five minutes before he was parking the car in the driveway in front of his small house.

He'd bought the small farm that butted up against Grant's property not long before their breakup, if it could be called that. Since then, Loralie had been noticeably absent from Ash Grove farm and had visited Kaitlyn

DuChamps-Ashworth much less frequently. He knew because he'd been watching for her small car every time he'd heard one pass his house.

Kaitlyn had gathered clothes and toiletries for Loralei earlier in the day and dropped them off, along with her own dire warnings and threats. It had been something akin to peeling his testicles like a grape. He hadn't said much in return. She was Loralei's friend, and given what a shit he'd been, she was entitled to hate him. Not a one of them could loathe him as much as he loathed himself. Hurting Loralei out of his own stupid pride and petty insecurity had been one of the lowest things he'd ever done.

No changing the past, he reminded himself as he took the keys from the ignition. He glanced at her from the corner of his eye. The place hadn't changed much since she'd been there last, but he'd managed to add a bit in the way of furnishings. He'd bought a new bed, mostly because he couldn't bear to sleep in the one he'd shared with her.

"It's never been the lap of luxury, but it'll do for the time being," he said.

"I liked your house, Ciaran. I liked it then, I like it now. The house was never the problem."

He tried to see it through her eyes. Compared to her home, it wasn't just modest but poor. Loralei had inherited her house from an aunt, and it was prime real estate in the downtown area and reflected the difference in their social status like nothing else. "Don't lie. It's a shit hole."

She glanced over her shoulder at him. "No. I don't say things I don't mean, Ciaran."

It was a direct hit, piercing the skin and digging deep. He'd meant everything he said to her except for the hateful words that had escaped him during their last argument. But those were the words she'd always remember. The minute he'd uttered them, he'd seen the hurt in her. He'd wanted to stop, to apologize then and try to repair the damage, but that ugly voice had been whispering in his head, *end it now, walk out on your own terms before she dumps you for someone else, you're not good enough*. It wasn't the first time those thoughts had pushed him into acting like a total shite.

"Come inside, then. I did at least shovel the dirty clothes out of your way," he said, his voice gruff with things he couldn't quite bring himself to express. Loralei had no idea just how special she was, and the worst part of it was, he'd done nothing to show her. If she doubted where she stood with him, he had no one but himself to blame.

It was mid-afternoon, and the bar was nearly deserted. Only a few patrons nursed their drinks, heads bowed over them. A few women danced on the stage, none of them making much effort. The people who were there wouldn't tip anyway. No one made eye contact with anyone else.

Sergei entered and immediately moved toward the only occupied table. In the back corner, two men sat at the table watching him approach. Their partner had instructed him not to kill the cop's sister, but he was not the only man Sergei answered to. Others had said she should die, and he feared them much more than the dirty cop.

Nervous, he touched the claw marks on his face and neck, courtesy of the fat bitch of a sister. Eliminate the woman, make it ugly enough to shift the cop's focus and teach him a lesson. Now, not only was the sister not dead, she was a witness who could tie it all together.

"I hope that dead bitch is lying in the morgue without her fingers," Ivanko said. "DNA evidence fucks everything up."

"She's not dead," Sergei admitted, taking the last remaining chair at the table.

Before he could seat himself fully, it was kicked from beneath him, and he sprawled on the floor. "Bastard!" Ivanko shouted.

Dimitri spoke then. "Enough from both of you! We did not come to this town to make spectacles of ourselves and act like fools for the locals. We brought our product here because it is an untapped market. All this is still true, even with the minor obstacle we have encountered. You have twenty-four hours, Sergei, to make this right. That is all our policeman can provide us. Twenty-five thousand does not buy loyalty, only rents it."

Sergei righted the chair and took his seat. "I will get her, Dimitri. I promise."

"I know you will. Now go and get yourself cleaned up."

Sergei rose and walked away. As he left, Ivanko looked at Dimitri. "That's it? You're going to just let him walk away? This could fuck us, Dimitri!"

Dimitri sipped his drink and paused thoughtfully. "No. Sergei is a threat now. He must be eliminated. I know where the girl is. Our rented policeman has been thorough. You will go with him. You will be certain the job is done. When you drive him out to the country, you do not drive him back. Understood?"

"And the girl?" Ivanko asked.

Dimitri shook his head. "We don't have time for dramatics. Make it quick. Just put a bullet in her with

Sergei's gun. We'll let Crawford stew in his grief and guilt because he failed to protect his sister."

Ivanko smiled. "It has been too long since you got your own hands dirty. You could come with us."

Dimitri took another sip. "I take no pleasure in the killing, only the spoils. Get it done, Ivanko."

Three

H ours later, settled in Ciaran's small house with a John Hughes marathon running on the television, Loralei glared at him from the couch. "I don't understand why we couldn't stay at my house! I have a business to run. I still need to go to the shop and try to put everything back together," she protested.

"And if your customers get shot while they're trying to buy one of your pretty dresses, you won't have a business left. As for your house—no security, no protection from the street, too many entrances and exits, and impossible for one man to secure," he replied, checking the windows and drawing the blinds. There was no point in advertising their presence.

"I don't think I can do this...I can't be locked up in here with you for days. Not without killing you or going crazy."

Ciaran smiled, but not in humor. The truth of the matter was, he felt the same. Loralei had gotten under his skin in a way no woman ever had. She thought he'd walked away because he didn't care, but it was just the opposite. He'd walked away because he cared too much, because she made him feel things and want things that he wasn't ready for. "You wouldn't be the first to try and put an end to me, but if you could manage it in your condition, I'd damn well deserve it."

She muttered something that sounded like "asshole" and then, with some difficulty, managed to stretch out on the couch. He didn't offer to help her. She'd made it abundantly clear that she didn't want him touching her. That hadn't always been the case. Memories of her overly feminine bedroom, draped in ruffles and lace, of Loralei stretched out on the bed, purring like a cat beneath his questing hands, clamored in his mind. But always, he'd left her alone, sneaking out into the night while she slept.

She'd never stayed overnight at his house simply because he never let anyone do that. The nightmares made him dangerous. Waking up in the darkness with another human being close to him wasn't a good idea. Having her in his home, guarding her twenty-four seven was a kind of enforced intimacy that could only lead to complications. But maybe it was time to complicate his life a little. Walking away from Loralei hadn't done a damn thing to erase her from his mind.

"You need to take your pills, or you'll wake up hurting," he reminded her gently.

She rolled her eyes. "I don't need you to tell me what to do!"

"Yes, you fucking do. You're only being hardheaded about this because I'm the one who said it. Good advice is good advice, Loralei, regardless of where it comes from. I'll get the pills, and I'll get you a drink, and you'll bloody well take them!"

As if she hadn't protested, he retrieved a Diet Coke

from the fridge, knowing it was her beverage of choice, and placed it next to her elbow along with the pill bottle. Churchill, a noble name for an ignoble beast, was snuggled on the back of the couch, panting as if he'd run a marathon. "I'll make us some dinner," he said. "Take the damn pill."

He walked away, headed for the kitchen. Her muttered curse followed him along with the sound of the rattling pill bottle. She might put up a fight for appearance's sake, but at the end of the day, she was nobody's fool.

Loralei, in spite of her silver-spoon upbringing, was a practical woman. Of course, the silver spoon had been yanked from her mouth fairly early on in life because her controlling bitch of a mother thought poverty would inspire Loralei to lose weight. He shook his head thinking about it. His own family, at least on his mother's side, had been fucked up. As for his father's family, they were an unknown quantity.

It was hard to imagine any family being as massively screwed up as the Crawfords and not have them imploding on daytime television. Matt was difficult to take, and Loralei had her share of issues, but as they'd been birthed and raised by a bloody iceberg, it was a miracle they weren't both locked up in the nuthouse.

The time he spent in the kitchen helped to calm his temper and give him back a bit of his hard-won control. She was in his head and under his skin. It wouldn't go well for either of them. But cooking, as always, helped. It reminded him of growing up on the small farm just outside Quin.

His grandmother hadn't held to the notion that a man shouldn't cook and clean up after himself. She'd put him to work, and he'd discovered he had an affinity and a

36

knack for cooking. It calmed his mind, soothed his ragged peace, and by the time the meal was done, he felt like he could face her again.

Filling two plates, he carried them into the living room. It was simple fair, roast chicken with potatoes and carrots, tasty without being too heavy for her. Given the amount of pain medication she was on, that was important. As he walked in, Churchill opened one eye, yawned loudly, and then promptly went back to snoring.

"Damned lazy beast," he muttered.

"An old Irish recipe?"

He laughed. "No. I think this might have been the Barefoot Contessa...or Martha Stewart. I can't recall for certain."

She frowned. "I just don't see you as the type to sit around watching cooking shows all day."

"I like to cook. My grandmother taught me the basics...but the fancier stuff I picked up while I was recuperating from a bullet. I was at this hospital in Germany, and one of the nurses was a fan of American cooking shows. She brought me what she had on tape while I was stuck there."

He'd never told her those kinds of things before, he realized. Every word out of his mouth had been guarded, every secret held close and tight. The fear that she'd reject him if she really knew him had created a chasm between them. No, he corrected. He had created a chasm between them. Looking at her, bruised and battered, but alive and once again within reach, he'd tell her anything she wanted to know if it meant he could just keep her.

He'd charmed her, no doubt, Loralei thought grimly. He was good at that. Turn on the charm and leave them wanting more. She stopped herself from saying anything to that effect. There was no way it wouldn't sound like petty jealousy, and she didn't want to give him the satisfaction.

"I didn't know you'd ever been shot," she said.

"You've seen the scar," he said, pointing to his side.

Recalling the wicked-looking chunk of missing flesh there, Loralei's eyes widened in horror. "What did they shoot you with? God above!"

He chuckled. "The scarring isn't from the bullet, love. It's from having to cauterize the wound in the field. We were too far away from our exit point, and I was bleeding too badly to go any further. If my buddies hadn't done that...well, someone else would have had to cook you dinner."

"Well, I'm glad you made it out," she replied, taking a bite of the chicken.

Another laugh escaped him. "You sound less than sure, *milish*."

"What does that mean? You said it last night."

He met her gaze steadily, his green eyes so deep and dark she could have drowned in them. After a charged second, she looked away, unable to maintain the contact as he spoke. "It's Gaelic. It means sweet."

It hadn't been so long ago that those kinds of endearments uttered in Gaelic would have set her heart pounding and had visions of white dresses and picket fences dancing in her head. Now, they hurt. They reminded her of dashed hopes and disappointment. "You shouldn't call me that...or love, or whatever that other word is that you call me. It can't be that way with us, Ciaran."

"I don't mean anything by it, Loralei. It's just a way of speaking," he said softly.

He didn't. He wouldn't. But everything he said and everything he did had far more significance to her than it ought, and if she was going to get out of her present situation with her sanity intact, it had to stop. She put her plate down and rose. "You never did, and now that I know that, it only makes it worse."

Leaving him staring after her, Loralei retreated to the bedroom he'd shown her earlier. It was his. She could get the faintest whiff of his cologne when she entered the room. She lay back on the large king-size bed and battled the urge to cry. All her emotions were running hot, just below the surface. The tiniest thing would set her off.

Matt's words came back to her, about the man who'd attacked her. He was right, she knew that, and taking her chances on her own didn't appeal. But the idea of having these repeated and charged encounters with Ciaran was more than she could handle. Rolling onto her side, she closed her eyes and tried to gather some control over her emotions. She had to reel it in, or she'd never survive the next few days.

"Please, Matt, figure this out and do it fast," she whispered.

Ciaran waited for half an hour for her to return, but she hadn't. Loralei wasn't a pouter. She didn't sulk and expect people to pander to her. If she left the room, it wasn't to make him come after her, but because she was done with looking at him. He put away the leftovers. If he put the lid on the container with a little more force than necessary, so be it. He slammed the refrigerator door so hard that all the contents rattled.

He wasn't angry so much as frustrated. She had every right to feel that way, to be livid with him. If the situation were different, she would never have spoken to him again and justifiably so. That moment, when he'd fucked it all up, replayed in his mind on a daily basis.

They'd been out at the bar with Kaitlyn and Grant, but the other couple had left early. He'd been in a rare mood, having finally worked up the courage to attempt contact with his long and apparently willingly lost father. To say it hadn't gone well was an understatement.

While he'd been at the bar, a man had approached Loralei. Embracing, laughing, clearly happy to see one another, when Ciaran had looked at them, he'd seen only one thing—the bastard was money, the same kind of money his father's family came from, the club that he was being excluded from. As he'd approached, Loralei had smiled at him, and then she'd made the introductions. He couldn't even recall the bastard's name except that he'd had about seven of them, and they were followed by the words "the third."

Ciaran leaned back against the kitchen counter. He'd been an asshole that night, accusing her of slumming it with the farm hand. He'd pushed her away, telling her that none of it had meant anything anyway, and it was time for her to go back with her own kind, that they'd been doing nothing more than killing time with one another anyway. Of course, it hadn't been that bloodless, nowhere near it.

He'd walked out of her house, slamming the door behind him, and they hadn't spoken since. Not until last night.

"Fuck me," he muttered, and strode down the hallway toward the bedroom. He knocked but didn't wait for an answer. She wouldn't give him one he liked anyway. Opening the door, he stepped into the room and stopped cold.

It hadn't occurred to him what it would do to him to

see her in his bed. She'd fallen asleep, her dark lashes resting against her cheeks and her chestnut brown hair disheveled. He had no name for whatever it was she was wearing, though she undoubtedly would. The woman loved clothes like he loved air. Whatever it was, he approved wholeheartedly. It draped over every curve, clinging to her lush body in a way that made his mouth go dry and his blood rush.

He stood there for a long moment, just drinking in the sight. A part of him couldn't stop imagining what it would be like to come in and find her like this every day, to know she was waiting for him at home, in bed, his. He was well and truly sunk, and he knew it.

Her eyes fluttered then drifted open. A soft smile curved her lips as if she'd forgotten for one small moment that he was an utter ass. It didn't last long. That smile faded and was quickly replaced with a frown and a furrowed brow. "What are you doing in here, Ciaran?"

I'm sorry. I was an ass. I put my foot in my mouth and say the wrong thing whenever I'm near you. I've missed you. I think about you every night and every morning and almost every minute in between. A dozen options ran through his mind, but as she sat up in the bed, still gazing expectantly at him, he knew nothing he could say would ever convey all he felt. Action had always been more his style.

Ciaran moved forward and gently cupped her face in his hands. Mindful of the dark bruise on her cheek, he traced it gently with his thumb. Her breath caught, and she stared up at him in confusion, but then he bent toward her, and as he did, her eyes fluttered closed. Ciaran settled his mouth over hers in the gentlest of kisses. It wasn't about the heat, though it burned inside him like always for her. With his lips playing over hers, molding to her softness, she sighed against him.

Placing one knee on the bed, Ciaran moved closer to her. The pug, who had been snoring loudly, gave a disapproving snort as he rose and toddled to the end of the bed. Neither of them noticed. Holding Loralei to him, he deepened the kiss. She hesitated for just a second then parted her lips for him, welcoming him in. The taste of her was more potent than whiskey. Dark, rich, tempting —he'd never forgotten it, but the memory couldn't do it justice.

Her hand came up, sliding over his back, pulling him close rather than pushing him away. It was a small victory, but he would take whatever he could get. Seizing the advantage, Ciaran eased her back on the bed. He wanted nothing more than to strip her clothes away and show her in the only way he knew how just how precious she was to him, but it was too much too soon. So, he contented himself with lying there with her, holding her, kissing her. It was so much more than he ever thought to have again.

When he could torment himself with it no more, his body burning for her like a bonfire, he eased back and met her questioning gaze. "I've been wanting to do that for two months now," he admitted gruffly.

"I don't understand how you can make me senseless with nothing more than a kiss. It isn't fair," she murmured.

"No, it isn't fair. None of this is," he agreed. "I never meant those things I said to you that night, Loralei, not a bloody one of them. I was jealous and mean with it."

The hurt and confusion he saw in her eyes cut him to the quick, but it was the mistrust in her voice that shamed him the most.

"We'd argued before," she reminded him. "You'd been

jealous before, but it was different...I could feel you pushing me away. You were so cold, and then when you said I was nothing more than a pastime, well...if you cared for me at all, you had a damned funny way of showing it."

He rolled onto his back and stared up at the ceiling, but he didn't let go of her. He held her close to his side and tried to figure out how to tell her what a small-minded prick he was. "Jealousy and insecurity are two sides of the same coin, love. I looked at that man you were talking to, a man with money and connections and a pedigree that I could never even come close to...and I could see the way he looked at me." It still stung, the dismissal, the slight disdain as if he hadn't been worth acknowledging. "Then there was your family. Your brother is right enough, but your mother looked at me like I was something dirty she'd stepped in."

Loralei gave a snort. "She looks at me that way half the time. I'm not my mother, and as you so eloquently put it in the past, I couldn't give two shits for her opinion."

He chuckled in spite of the serious nature of their conversation. Hearing Loralei use his crude idioms amused him. It was half the reason he uttered them in front of her to begin with. "I'm not good enough for you. I never bloody was. It's one thing for me to know it, for you to know it, and even for your monster of a mother to know it. It was another for that bastard to look at me like I'm a fucking servant who forgot his place."

She huffed out an exasperated breath. "For the love of God! Jameson Beech is just a boy I went to school with!"

"He's not a boy, Loralei. He's a grown man, and he clearly thinks of you as a grown woman!"

"He's a boy to me," she replied softly. "Spoiled and used to having his own way, defined by his car and his clothes and by the money his ancestors managed to amass...but he'll never be half the man you are. Can't you see that?"

He didn't look at her, but he did smile. "All I see is that you could do a damn sight better than me or that bastard. You deserve a man who can give you a house and a nice car, who can go to the kinds of parties you do and not stick out like a sore thumb. I'll never be that kind of man, Loralei. I'll always be the Irish farm hand."

"I never wanted you to be anything else," she said simply.

"I should never have said what I did. It wasn't true. You've always been more to me than that. You have to know that."

She lay back on the bed, her head on the pillow next to his as they looked up at the ceiling together. "No. I don't know that. You see all the men with money and fifteen first names as being a better choice than you, and I see every woman who is fifty pounds lighter than me as being better. Neither of us is perfect, Ciaran, but for a minute, I thought maybe we were perfect for each other. What happens the next time I run into a friend from school? Or my mother, God forbid, tries to set me up with someone she deems appropriate?"

The hurt in her voice cut right through him, but he had no chance to reply. He heard the crunch of wheels on gravel a split second before the beam of too-bright headlights spilled through the window.

He didn't think or question, but grabbed her and rolled her off the bed with him just as a spray of bullets ripped through the windows and the siding, tearing holes in everything and showering them with splinters of wood and glass.

The dog yelped with fright and huddled under the bed, having taken cover at the first sign of trouble. Clearly the wee beast was smarter than he'd given him credit for. The spray of bullets was endless. Everything he owned was being torn to shreds around them.

Loralei screamed, and he shushed her, his mouth close to her ear. "Be quiet, love. I need you under the bed now. Go."

She did as he asked, scooting under the bed though it undoubtedly caused her pain. The jolt off the bed had done no favors for her either. He could see blood on the carpet where her stitches had torn open. The pug trembled against her side, wide-eyed and terrified.

Cursing the bastards outside and wanting a little blood of his own, Ciaran crawled on his elbows until he could reach the nightstand. Rather than reach up, he opened the bottom drawer and placed his hand under the top drawer, working it until it crashed to the floor. He had two handguns inside it. He gave the smaller of the two to Loralei. "It's loaded. Can you fire it?"

"My brother is a cop! I'm from Kentucky, for heaven's sake!"

Her reply prompted a wicked grin. "Right, then. If you see any boots but these," he said, pointing to his scuffed cowboy boots, "put a bullet in them. Aim for the big toe. You hit it, and those fuckers won't even be able to see."

She nodded and flipped the safety off. It was surprisingly sexy to watch her handling a gun. Making a mental note to revisit that later, Ciaran rose into a crouch and began making his way out of the bedroom. He didn't go to the door but lifted the edge of the rug in the hallway and opened the trap door there. It was an old habit from his army days, but he always liked to have an exit that was unknown.

Lowering himself into the crawl space, he closed the

door behind him, the weighted carpet falling into place. Just to the left of the porch, he positioned himself behind a cement column for cover and began firing shots through the lattice work there.

Ciaran took careful aim, each shot measured and considered. His first shot took out a tire, and with his second, he took out a knee. He didn't know Russian, but he knew curses. The shooter retreated into the lame truck and took off down the drive, sparks flying off the exposed rim. Still, he waited. They could double back, or they could have left someone behind to pick them off unawares.

When the stairs above him didn't creak, when the house settled into the silence, and more to the point when the night sounds from the surrounding woods resumed, he climbed out from under the porch and made his way back to Loralei.

"It's me," he called out. "Don't shoot me, or if you do, at least leave me with my dignity."

She peered out from beneath the bed. Her face was white with fear. "How did they find me here, Ciaran?"

It was a damn good question. "We're having a talk with your brother, and we'll find out."

Sergei screamed as the truck dipped onto the shoulder again, and his leg shifted. The kneecap was shattered. He didn't have to look to know that. "I'll kill that Irish fuck," he groaned.

"You haven't managed to kill a mere woman...one who makes a generous target at that!" Ivanko snarled, struggling to keep the truck on the pavement. They reached the parking lot of an all-night drugstore, and he swerved the truck into a parking space.

"Why the fuck are you stopping?" Sergei shouted. "I need a doctor!"

Ivanko pulled his handgun from his jacket, the silencer on the end leaving no question about his intentions, and pointed it at Sergei. "No, my friend, you don't." He squeezed the trigger, the bullet ripping through the other man's head and burrowing into the seat beneath him. Blood and tissue spattered the windows, but they were tinted so darkly, no one outside would see it, at least not until daylight.

Getting out of the truck, he straightened his clothes and walked away from the vehicle and the corpse of a man he'd known for two decades. He would need to report to Dimitri that they had failed, and he would need to discover why their information had not included the fact that the Irishman was more than just a civilian. Whoever he fucking was, he had skills that only came from years of training.

Four

Ciaran was waiting for Matt when he entered the house. It was riddled with bullet holes, and half his furniture was in shreds. More importantly, one of Loralei's wounds had partially reopened in their tumble from the bed. The paramedics were seeing to it.

"Who the hell have you been talking to?" Matt demanded.

Ciaran raised his eyebrows at that. "I've not talked to a fucking soul, you bastard! Who the hell have you told that she was here?"

Matt shook his head. "Grant knows, so does Kaitlyn, but neither of them will say anything. Hell, our own mother doesn't even know where she is, though to be fair, that's more because she's with you than because of the situation."

"And the cops?" Ciaran asked sharply. "How many of them knew where she was hiding?"

Matt bristled at that. "My people aren't dirty!"

"Clearly someone is! Think about it, would you?

Within four hours of her leaving the hospital and getting settled in here, and the fucking shooter is out front, guns blazing? You tell me how that adds up!"

Matt stepped back. "I can't. I don't have the answer!"

"You don't want to accept the answer," Ciaran declared. "It is what it is. I've said nothing, and I'd trust Grant before I'd trust a bunch of underpaid cops. Kaitlyn would go to her grave before she'd sell Loralei out...that leaves your bunch."

Matt didn't reply, just moved past him to where Loralei was having her ankle bandaged by the paramedic. "Jesus, Lor, can't you stay out of trouble for five minutes?"

She was unamused, giving him a baleful stare. "Really? I'm in this mess because you can't stay out of trouble! And now Ciaran is in the middle of it too! What the hell, Matt? Who are these guys, and how do you stop them?"

He crouched in front of her. "I'm close. I swear to you, I am. I just need a day...two at most, and I'll have their asses locked up, and you can go back to your normal life."

Loralei glared at him, and her voice, when she spoke, was somewhere between pissed off and mildly hysterical. "Normal! My shop is in ruins, I've been stabbed, and now I've been shot at! There is no normal after this, Matt! I've nearly died twice in just as many days!"

"Ciaran," he began, but had to clear his throat as it galled him to admit it. "Ciaran thinks there could potentially be a leak in the department."

She was focused on watching the paramedic tape the bandage over her ankle. "And what do you think about that?"

Matt rocked back on his heels, put his hands in his

pocket, and stared at the toes of his shoes. "I'm thinking there might be something to the theory. I've got to look into some things, but I might be able to provide just enough misinformation to make sure whoever is behind this hangs in their own noose. Do you trust me?"

"After today? I'm reconsidering, but we'll go with this one on account." Her sarcasm was so thick it would have taken an idiot to miss it. "You're my big brother. Of course, I trust you. Your coworkers are another story altogether."

"Walk me through what happened here," he said.

"Ciaran and I were in the bedroom—"

"And you think my judgment isn't sound?" he asked incredulously. "That guy did a number on you, Lor, like no one else ever has. It took him less than five hours to get you in bed!"

She rolled her eyes. "I said we were in the bedroom, Matt, not that we were in bed. Get your mind out of the gutter! We were talking. That's all!" It wasn't a lie, she reasoned. At the time the first shot was fired, they had been just talking. "Ciaran heard the tires on the driveway and dragged me off the bed and to the floor before the bullets started flying. He had me hide under the bed, with a gun, and then went off to play hero...which I'm going to kick his ass for when I'm able."

"You can't kick his ass. Not ever. I'm not even sure I could kick it with Grant's help!"

"What the hell does that mean?" she demanded. "My head hurts, Matt, and I've had the ever-loving shit scared out of me twice! I can't do cryptic."

"I dug a little deeper into his service file with the help of a friend who ignored things like security clearance," Matt admitted. "The guy is good, Loralei. Not just good, but epic. Like the Celtic version of Rambo. He's a bonafide Irish Chuck Norris, for fuck's sake."

Loralei considered that information for a second, but it honestly didn't surprise her. Ciaran was always watchful, always aware of everything going on around them, and the few times she had seen him get physical with anyone, he'd moved in a way that just left her shaking her head. Precise, controlled, and wickedly efficient. "I kind of figured that out when he army crawled out of the house to take on the gunmen. Where do we go now?"

"You and he are going to figure that out. I'm out of it." Matt stepped closer to her, close enough to whisper without being overheard. "There are only two guys who knew where you were who I don't trust implicitly, and until today, I never would have questioned either one of them. One of them will be told you've gone back to your house. The other will be told you all are laying low at my apartment. Depending on where the bad guys show up, we'll know who our leak is."

"Do you really think that will work?"

Matt nodded. "These guys, the Russians, are out of pocket. They don't have the protection or backup of a family behind them. They're good, but they're alone. I'll get 'em, and I'll damn well end this. That's a promise."

Loralei rose and hugged him. "Thank you for being a truly amazing and kick-ass brother in every sense of the word."

"Don't get sentimental on me. You know that shit makes it weird," he said, backing up. As he did, he tugged at her messy ponytail, the remnants of a bun from earlier, in a gesture that was so reminiscent of their late father, it brought tears to her eyes.

"Never. Go. Figure this shit out so I can have my

house back, and Churchill won't require years of therapy."

He rolled his eyes. "That damn dog is a menace. I had to go to your house this morning and clean up about six piles. Kaitlyn wouldn't do it. What the hell do you feed him?"

"It's not what I feed him, it's what he scavenges. He's so low to the ground that he just finds all the stuff people drop and he shouldn't have. I had to stop walking him past that Mexican place on Vine. We were both miserable for days after he hoovered up the leavings there."

Matt grimaced. "Jesus." He leaned in and kissed the top of her head. "Be careful, and as much as it pains me to say it, do what Ciaran tells you to. If anybody can keep them from getting to you, it'll be him."

Loralei stood there, staring after him as he went to talk to the crime scene techs. Ciaran approached her, holding her overnight bag and Churchill's pet carrier. His own bag was slung over his shoulder.

"We need to go," he said softly.

Her eyes teared up, and she glanced at him. "They destroyed your house, Ciaran. I'm so sorry."

"They're just walls, *milish*. They can be rebuilt easily enough. You can't. Now get your beastie, and let's get you somewhere safe."

Loralei picked up Churchill and snuggled him close. She placed a kiss on the top of his fuzzy head and followed Ciaran out into the night.

Ciaran held the door of the borrowed truck for her. His own was shot to hell, all four tires flattened and not a window left intact. The fuckers, he thought bitterly. Wrecking a man's house was one thing, but destroying his truck was another altogether. Still, the truck Grant had provided for them at Matt's request was a step up. He could appreciate the sleek lines and cushy interior.

After she'd climbed in, he reached over her and fastened her seatbelt for her before walking around the vehicle and climbing behind the wheel. Leaving the remnants of his house behind, he turned onto the main road and headed toward town. He'd made a call to a friend who was out of the country and had been given the access code to his farm and the small cabin there that served as a guest house.

"Matt looked at your service record," she said abruptly.

It didn't surprise him. If he was entrusting someone with seeing to his sister's safety, he'd want to be damn sure he knew they were capable. He glanced over at her, "I never imagined he wouldn't."

"So just how bad-ass are you?"

Ciaran laughed. "I did ten years as a Ranger in the Irish Army...Special Forces with training similar to what your operatives would have here."

"I don't know what that means. Can you kill a man with your bare hands? Do you know seventeen deadly uses for a stick of gum? What?"

"I know only one or two truly good uses for a stick of gum. I can and have killed men with my bare hands, though I prefer not to."

She blanched, her face going pale. "I guess it's worse when you're that close to them."

He glanced over at her, his hands draped casually over the steering wheel of the borrowed truck. "Not really. Killing is killing, whether they're two feet from you or two hundred. But when you're that close, there are more chances for it to go wrong and for you to go down with them."

He said it so dispassionately, like he was talking about rebuilding an engine or how to debone a chicken. "Oh," she said.

Ciaran's heavy sigh told her she'd done a poor job of concealing just how much his answers had unnerved her. He didn't look at her again, but she had no doubt he was cataloging her every response.

When he finally spoke, his words were soft but earnest. "There's a reason we never talked about all this... yes, it is classified, but that part of my life is over. I never intended to use any of those skills again, but I don't regret anything I did then because it puts me in the unique position of being able to protect you now. And I will. No matter what."

It went quiet in the truck, both of them focused on what he'd just said. Finally, he sighed again. "There's something I need to tell you, and you probably won't like it, but it's been heavy on my mind," he offered with a shrug.

It was a familiar gesture, one he often used when uncomfortable or defensive. Immediately, Loralei was on alert, waiting for the backpedaling, the "it's not you, it's me, and this can't happen again" speech. "If it's going to piss me off or make me cry, I'd appreciate it if you just shelved it because I don't think I can handle another downward swing on today's roller coaster."

He glanced up at her then, his eyes widening in surprise. Then he shook his head. "I deserve that, I guess. You've more reasons not to trust me than to...but no, I don't think it'll do either of those things. And for the record, nothing that has ever passed between us, except my walking out, has ever been a mistake."

Unable to express her relief, Loralei gave a stiff nod. In the close quarters of the truck, close enough to smell him, to feel the heat of his body, she felt strangely vulnerable, perhaps because whatever he felt he needed to say had the power to utterly destroy her. But she'd never been a coward and had no intention of taking the easy way out. Head on, she decided. "So what is it then?"

He gripped the steering wheel more tightly, his knuckles white on it. A muscle worked in his jaw, clenching and unclenching until at last he spoke. "I didn't tell you the truth about why I came to Kentucky. There's a reason for that, and it relates here."

At the end of her patience and on pins and needles waiting for him to just spill whatever it was that he felt he needed to tell her, Loralei snapped at him. "You think maybe you could get to the point before daylight? The more you talk right now the less you say, and it's making me antsy as hell."

He chuckled. "God above, you've a temper like a wet cat! Here it is then. I've given you my apology and a partial explanation for what happened—for my own shitty mood and shittier treatment of you. But not all of it. I left something out that, truth be told, I was ashamed to confess."

A wave of nausea and fear rolled through her. "Was there another woman?"

He shook his head and gave her a shaming glance. "No, there hasn't been since the first night I laid eyes on you, and I've no mind to change that now. This—it's about my family."

Relief was instantaneous, washing through her in a flood. But on the heels of it, came distrust. Clearly, he'd been less than honest with her. "You told me you didn't have a family, other than your sister in New York," she said, her voice tinged with the hint of accusation.

"That's still true enough," he said, his voice chilled and biting. She never questioned that his anger was directed at her. In that moment, relating his story, she wasn't even sure he was totally aware of her presence. After several moments, he finally spoke again, "The truth of the matter is that I have a family, but they want no part of me. The day of our fight, I met my father."

Loralei frowned. "What do you mean 'met?'"

"He's from here, from Kentucky," Ciaran explained. "That was why I chose to come here...but it took a bit to work up the courage to go and see him. Suffice to say, it didn't go well."

"Okay," she said. "That's a starting point, but you do realize you need to offer a few more details than that, right?" It was like pulling teeth to get it out of him, and that was enough to tell her it was bad. Ciaran was more of a talker than most of the men in her acquaintance, but she attributed that to his Irish upbringing and a general, cultural love of storytelling. Still, it was unlike him to skirt the point so broadly.

He pulled the truck off to the side and put it in park, turning to look at her. His expression was utterly flat, devoid of emotion, and yet all the more evocative for it. Whatever had happened that day, he'd shut it down so fast that he hadn't even allowed himself a chance to feel it. Immediately, perhaps even instinctively, she knew it had been bad. Her urge to reach out to him was difficult to tamp down, but she didn't second guess herself on doing so. Offering him sympathy would only piss him off. Instead, she sat silently and waited.

Ciaran kept the truck in park, hands on the wheel, and stared out at the night as he told her the rest of it. "I went to his office at the distillery, told him who I was, and he told me to get my arse off his property before he called security. That I'd never see a penny of his, and if I thought I'd blackmail him over his past indiscretions, he'd see me in hell first."

Her heart broke for him in that moment, shattered into a million tiny pieces. She knew what it felt like to be rejected by a parent, but never so completely. Through the pain and the well of anger at such blatant cruelty, something else finally struck her. "Distillery...Samuel Darcy is your father?"

His expression hardened, his eyes going cold and dark. "Samuel Darcy is the Yank who slept with my mother and left her. I'll not call the bastard my father ever again. When I was in his office, I saw a picture of a group of young girls standing on the deck of a sailboat. You were one of them."

Loralei slumped against the seat, the weight of that pronouncement sinking into her. Everything was getting more and more tangled by the minute. "I'm friends with Mia...your sister," she said softly, though she didn't doubt for a moment he was already aware of it.

"She's not my sister. That was made more than clear to me, *milish*," he said sadly. "I'm not welcome here, at least not by them. The question is, how do you feel knowing I'd be a blight to you here?"

"What the hell does that mean?"

He shifted the truck into drive and pulled forward. Once the truck was in motion, he reached over and took her hand, holding it loosely in his. "It means that if you were to be with me, beyond this mess that's sprung up around you, it wouldn't go well for you. People you've known your whole life would most likely turn their backs on you."

Loralei unfastened her seatbelt and scooted toward him. On the gravel road, traveling at ten miles an hour, it was a safety risk she felt she could afford to take. Laying her head on his shoulder, she just savored the point of contact, the ability to touch him. "If they're small-minded enough to do that, then I don't need them in my life."

"And me? Do you need me in your life?" he asked.

"No," she answered honestly. "I don't need you in it. I want you in it."

He smiled up at her. "I think that might be better."

"But Ciaran, you have to promise me one thing."

"I'd promise you anything," he said and there was a wealth of meaning in his tone.

"You can't let what Samuel Darcy said color your perception of the rest of them. I can promise you he does not speak for the Darcys. His children hate him...Mia most of all. She has good reason. You need to meet her."

He pressed a kiss to the top of her head even as he turned off one gravel path and onto another. This one led to a gated entrance. "Is that really what you want to talk about right now? A sister who may or may not want anything to do with me?"

It was a topic they would revisit, she decided. "Whose place is this?" she asked.

Five

Without a word, Ciaran got out and opened the gate then came back to drive the truck through. Afterward, he got out and locked the gate behind him, setting the alarm on it. She didn't move from her spot as he returned to the truck and drove down the path.

When they reached the end of the long drive, he took a gravel road that veered off into the trees. The guest house was a log cabin that had been original to the property and had been restored.

"Come on. Inside with you and that...I hesitate to even call it a dog."

"You love Churchill!" she protested.

"I tolerate Churchill because you come as a pair," he said. "That dog produces more gas than some continents." As if to prove his point, the dog chose that moment to yawn widely, which in turn produced a particularly noxious fart. "Jesus!"

Loralei was laughing while holding her nose. "He does require a certain level of understanding and patience."

"Or the lack of a sense of smell," he agreed, reaching for their bags. He ushered her toward the cabin and retrieved the key from its hiding place on the beam above porch swing. After he unlocked the door and she'd gone inside, he glanced behind them, scanning the trees for anything that seemed off. He noted where the densest of shadows were, where branches twisted and mingled to create natural pockets a person could hide in. Satisfied he had the lay of the land, he entered the cabin behind her.

It was one large room with a small kitchenette and a living area. The far corner contained a large bed and opposite it was a bathroom encased in frosted glass. It was clearly a space intended for a single person or a couple who were very comfortable with one another.

"This is cozy," she said. By cozy she clearly meant awkward as hell.

He chuckled. "I've watched you shower up close without even the benefit of glass between us."

She moved toward the bed and sat down heavily on the edge of it. "Things were different then."

"They could be again...would already be if we hadn't been interrupted earlier," he reminded her as he placed their bags on the small bench at the foot of the bed. There was no closet, just an open shelving system along the wall. "But for now, I think you should eat something. You didn't have dinner, and you're looking a bit pale."

"I've been stabbed and shot at. It doesn't exactly put roses in your cheeks," she retorted smartly. "I'm not really hungry, and it isn't like I can't stand the loss of a few pounds."

"Don't do that," he warned. "Don't say things like that. There's nothing wrong with your weight or your body, other than what it's been put through in the last few days. You need to eat so you can heal. The kitchen's supposed to be stocked. I'll make you something."

She frowned at him. "You really don't think I'd look better thinner?"

He walked toward her, cupped her face in his hands and lifted her chin until they were eye to eye. "Loralei, I think you'd look better naked, but beyond that, there's no room for improvement in my book."

"I could be," she replied huskily. "Naked, that is." Her eyes had darkened with desire, and even in the dim light, he could see the hard points of her nipples through the thin, clinging fabric of her shirt. "I'm not hungry for food, Ciaran."

His whole body caught fire. "What are you hungry for, *mavourneen*?"

She reached for him, her hands fisting the fabric of his shirt as she tugged him toward her. "Just you."

He wanted to ask her if she was sure, he wanted to be the kind of man who'd consider the fact that she'd been through hell and might not be making good decisions. But he wasn't. He couldn't be that man with her. With her, he was greedy. He wanted her, wanted what she offered, and he was just needy enough himself to ignore his conscience. The taste of her, the feel of her soft skin against his, of her soft curves beneath him, had haunted him for the last two months.

He kissed her, molding his lips to hers. Her hands came up to rest on his shoulders, then splayed over his back as she pulled him closer. As he nipped gently at her bottom lip, she gasped, and it was the only invitation he needed. Sweeping his tongue between her softly parted lips, each stroke was a slow, sensual dance, an imitation of the act to follow.

Ciaran pressed her back onto the bed and followed

her down. They were still fully clothed, but their bodies touched from head to toe, pressed, held, strained against one another. It was, by equal turns, satisfying and frustrating. He wanted her naked against him, but he'd have to let go of her first in order to make that happen. As if she'd read his mind, her hands were at his shirt, tugging at it, bunching the fabric upward until her palms connected with skin. They skimmed over his sides, his back, her touch like a brand.

His own hands took a similar journey, delving beneath her clothes, skimming over the soft mound of her belly, his fingertips tracing the curve of her waist, moving upward until he encountered the lace of her bra. Cupping her breast, teasing the budded nipple through fabric, he pulled his lips from hers to kiss along her jawline, down her neck. When he reached the spot, the one just below her ear that always made her wild, he bit down, scraping his teeth over the sensitive skin as she gasped his name and arched beneath him.

"God, you make me crazy," she uttered breathlessly.

"Too many clothes," he murmured against her neck. "I need to feel your skin against mine."

She pressed against him, pushing him back just enough that she could reach for the hem of her shirt. Rather than let her do it, he stilled her hands with his and then brushed them aside. He pushed the fabric upward, freeing one arm and the other before pulling it over her head and tossing it aside. His gaze was drawn immediately to the white bandage at her shoulder. There were bruises all over her body, small marks here and there that were a vivid reminder of what had almost happened...twice.

"I don't want to think about that right now," she said, once again plucking the thoughts right from his mind. "I don't want to think at all."

A slight smile curved his lips as he reached for the waistband of her leggings and began working them down, over her hips and her thighs. "Let me see if I can't help you with that."

"Just hurry, for the love of God!"

He removed the rest of her clothes and her shoes, leaving her in only a pair of black lace panties and a matching bra. He stopped then, sitting back on his heels just to drink in the sight of her.

Bandages and bruises aside, which he couldn't let himself think about without becoming furious, she was perfect. Loralei thought because she wasn't thin, she couldn't be sexy, but when he looked at her full breasts, the gentle curve of her waist, and the flare of her hips, he saw only perfection. He'd lost count of the number of times she'd complained about the size of her thighs or cellulite or stretch marks or any of the other things she perceived as flaws. Meanwhile, he could only think of how good it felt to have those lush thighs pressed against him, her long legs wrapped around him, to feel the softness of her flesh under his hands.

"Why would I hurry a moment I'd like to last forever?" he asked, one hand roaming over the curve of her hip, down her thigh to the back of her knee. She squirmed, just as he'd known she would.

Her hands did their own roaming at that point, raking along his sides until she could hook her fingers into his belt loops and tug him closer. As her fingers reached for his belt buckle, he knew then that he was lost. She'd have it and him her way, just as she always did, because he was helpless to resist her.

Brushing her hands away, he completed the task for her. With one tug, he sent his shirt flying across the room. He rose from the bed just long enough to remove his boots and shed his jeans, a task he completed in record time. Then he was on the bed with her again, skin to skin, their bodies touching with the promise of what was to come.

"I don't want you to regret this later," he murmured softly. "We've enough regrets between us already."

"The only thing I regret is wasting time. I pouted and whined because you didn't call me, but I didn't make an effort to reach out to you either," she confessed as her hands coasted along his back, her nails raking along his skin in a way that always drove him wild.

"I wanted to apologize. A hundred times I picked up my phone and then changed my mind. I wanted to tell you the truth then, about my father and everything else... but I never wanted to see that pitying look in your eye. But we're here now." He punctuated those statements with soft kisses along her collarbone, the tender skin of her neck, the curve of her shoulder which had always lured him.

"So now that you've got me naked, do you think you could do something besides talk my ear off?"

Her sharp words prompted a chuckle from him. As his breath fanned over her skin, she shivered beneath him. Her response effectively ended his amusement, the mood suddenly becoming far more serious.

"Tell me what you want, *mavourneen*, and I'll be happy to give it to you."

Loralei felt the weight of his body on hers, the hot press of his skin, and the skilled touch of his hands as they roamed over her body. "I want you," she answered simply.

He kissed her again, his lips moving over hers in a way that left her breathless and weak. All the while, his hands roamed her body, touching her everywhere, sometimes gently and sometimes bordering on rough, but always, it was just what she needed. Every touch was designed to inflame, to drug her senses and leave her wanting more.

As his lips left hers, burning a path along her jaw, over the tender skin of her throat, she gave a startled yelp when his teeth scraped there, just forcefully enough to sting. But the soothing sweep of his tongue over her flesh prompted a moan and then a sigh as she held him close, her fingers twined in his dark hair as if to hold him to her. It was an illusion. No one would hold Ciaran unless he wanted them to, but in that moment, anchoring him to her in such a way made her feel whole and alive like she hadn't since he'd left.

Then his mouth was at her breasts, teasing and taunting her through the satin and lace of her bra. He played with the hardened peaks of her nipples. First one and then the other was treated to the warm pull of his lips and the soft rasp of his tongue. It was followed with the firm pressure of his fingers, taking her to that ephemeral place between pleasure and pain. It was all yearning and eagerness and consuming need.

"Ciaran, please!" she urged as her hands left his hair to roam over his back. Her nails scored his skin and some part of her reveled in causing him that little bit of pain. "You're killing me."

He smiled, but there was a tension in his face, in the tight line of his jaw and the clenching of his muscles. It told the truth of just how much it cost him to let the fire build in a slow, controlled burn rather than an all-consuming inferno. Hoping to urge him along, she reached for the clasp of her bra but winced as the movement pulled at her stitches.

"Let me," he said and stilled her hands. He sat up, lifted her against him, cradling her against his chest as he quickly disposed of the garment. Then he laid her back on the bed again. He remained sitting, his eyes raking over her body.

The weight of his stare was like a touch—hot, heavy, and painfully arousing. Her nipples tightened further, furling into taut, aching buds that begged for his touch. A soft sigh escaped her as he dipped his head to take one in his mouth. Without the impeding fabric between them, the heat of his mouth was scorching. His touch was surprisingly gentle, but heightened as her nerves already were, it took only the slightest pressure to have her writhing against him. She wanted to feel him inside her, to have his hardness filling her up and easing the ache that had settled low in her belly.

Her hands roamed his back, his sides, tracing the ridged indentations of his abs, and then moved lower. When her fingers encountered the thick, hard ridge of his cock, she gripped him firmly with her fingers but traced slow, lazy circles with her thumb. "Don't make me wait anymore, Ciaran."

He didn't make her ask twice. He moved away from her questing hands just long enough to shed the dark boxers he wore. When he came back down onto the bed, he hooked his thumbs beneath the elastic band of her panties and worked them slowly over her hips, careful of her injuries. Once they were both completely naked, he urged her onto her side and moved behind her. She could feel the hard press of his erection against her bottom as he draped her thigh over his.

"Those stitches," he said, his fingers tracing the edge

of the bandage, "Have taken enough of a beating tonight."

"I just want to feel you inside me...I don't give a damn how you make it happen," she said, arching against him.

His head dropped, and he brushed a gentle kiss to her shoulder as he shifted slightly. The head of his cock nudged at the slick seam of her sex. He moved against her, teasing her, sliding over her damp flesh, but never seeking entrance. A shattered moan escaped her, and it was all the encouragement he needed. He pressed more fully, parting her flesh, sinking into her in one long, slow push.

Loralei uttered his name on a gasp and pressed back against him, taking him deeper. With Ciaran, it had always been wild, unfettered, bordering on a violent free-for-all as they wrestled all over the bed and tried to best one another. But this was different. Hindered by her injuries, careful not to cause further harm, they came together slowly, their bodies rocking gently against one another. His hands moved over her breasts, her hips, in soft, gentle strokes.

Loralei pressed against him, savoring the heat and the sweat that slicked their skin. His mouth moved to her neck, his lips and teeth teasing her flesh as he surged into her again and again.

Their breathing became labored, their movements more fierce, but the deep connection she felt to him, cradled against him as he carried them both to the edge, was unlike anything she'd ever felt. Her thighs trembled and her belly quivered as the pleasure built. She cried out as she peaked, her muscles clenching rhythmically as he pressed deeper into her. His body tensed against her, a shudder racked him, and then he followed her over that knife's edge of pleasure.

In the aftermath, neither of them spoke. For the

moment, they were cocooned in their own little world, in the pleasure that had been given and taken in one another. His arms closed around her, holding her to him, and she snuggled against the hard wall of his chest, content for the moment to simply savor the closeness and let their convoluted history simmer in the background. She'd take what she could, and when he walked away from her again, as she was certain he would, she'd be strong enough to watch him do it with her head held high. At the very least, she'd be strong enough to fake it.

Six

Matt stared at the screen of his laptop with bleary eyes. He'd been awake for more than twenty-four hours, and at least twenty of those hours had been pure hell.

"Burning the midnight oil, Crawford?"

Matt looked up to see Jenkins walking toward his desk. He was relatively new to the force, transferred in from Western Kentucky. He was also one of the prime suspects in leaking the information about Loralei's whereabouts. "This mess with my sister is making me crazy...if I don't get it figured out soon, I'm gonna lose it."

Jenkins nodded as he refilled his coffee cup. "Heard about the boyfriend's place getting shot up. That's a real clusterfuck. Any leads?"

"Our drug dealer in custody has suddenly decided that there really is honor among thieves...he's clammed up as tight as Fort Knox. I have a string of Russian first names and a couple of bars where they might be holed up, but no luck pinning them down anywhere, so far."

Jenkins nodded again. "Too bad you can't just beat it out of him."

Matt chuckled in response. "Yeah. It's not the Wild West anymore."

"Your sister safe for now?" Jenkins asked.

The opportunity had literally fallen into his lap, which made Matt even more suspicious. "Yeah. She and Ciaran are laying low at my apartment for now...but that's just between us."

"Not a problem, man. I'll keep it quiet. I'm heading out to get some sleep. You should too. You look like hell."

"As soon as these reports are done...hell, I might crash here. Better than being a third wheel in my own damn house," Matt joked.

Jenkins chuckled. "I hear that," he agreed as he walked away.

When the man was out of sight, Matt closed his computer and grabbed his keys and jacket. Heading out the back door, he climbed behind the wheel of Kaitlyn's little sports car. She was a pain in the ass, but she had amazing taste in automobiles. It was the flashiest under-cover vehicle he'd ever been in, that was for damn sure.

The drive to his apartment didn't take long. While Lexington traffic was a beast in the daytime, at night the city went dead quiet. Rather than let himself in, he settled down to watch and wait. Grant, on a recon basis only, was watching Loralei's house, staked out in his mother's Volvo. Alvarez, the other cop who had yet to be vetted, had been told that Loralei and Ciaran had returned to her house not long before his conversation with Jenkins.

Taking his cell from his pocket, Matt tapped the speed dial number for Grant. "Anything?" he asked immediately.

"A skunk," Grant replied. "Two opossums. A couple

of drunken frat boys and a homeless guy who pissed on someone's shiny new Beemer."

Matt grinned. "Please tell me it was the door handle. That shit makes my day."

"It was," Grant said, and there was a note of glee in his voice. "Call me crazy. I haven't seen fuck-all here, Matt. Are you sure Alvarez is dirty?"

"No. But I'm not certain he isn't, and I can't take any chances with Loralei...she's all I've got. Well, except for you and your wife, who I think might actually have warmed up to me."

Grant chuckled. "Kaitlyn doesn't do warm, Matt. Hate to break it to you. She tolerates you, but that's pretty much her stance on all humans over the age of fifteen. But she hasn't chewed your ass yet, so you might be on her good side. If she has one."

Matt shook his head. Kaitlyn DuChamps-Ashworth was like a badger trapped in a supermodel's body. Vicious and beautiful all at the same time, but she'd move heaven and earth for Loralei, so she was okay in his book.

"Fuck," Grant said softly. "A car just pulled up in front of Loralei's house. Dark tinted windows, late model Escalade, two guys getting out while the third keeps the engine running."

"Stay down, don't let them see you," Matt said and started the car.

Grant sighed. "I think it's too late for that. One of the guys just pointed this way and shouted something in Russian."

"Get out. Put that fucking mom-mobile in gear and get the fuck out."

Matt could hear the revving of the engine and the squealing of tires.

"They're right on me, Matt," Grant said. "I'm

heading toward campus. I can lose them down some of those side streets maybe."

Matt gripped the wheel tighter as he sped off toward Loralei's house. "Find a fucking cop...even a damn campus rent-a-cop!"

He heard the sound of breaking glass, and then nothing. The call had been disconnected. Speed dialing dispatch, he identified himself and began barking commands.

In the upstairs bedroom of Loralei's house, Dimitri closed the laptop. The idiot woman needed better security and stronger passwords. The framed photo of her ugly dog bearing his name had been a dead giveaway to the password of her computer. Now, he'd managed to track the location of her phone by reporting it "lost," which had the added benefit of turning it off entirely. If she attempted to use it, it would simply give her an out of service message.

Ivanko had taken care of the cop's friend, albeit temporarily. Still, it would give the cop something else to worry about while they tracked down his little sister. There was a slim chance the cop might figure out why they had taken the other man's phone and warn the Irishman, but it was a risk they had to take.

"Let's move," Dimitri said, rising quickly to his feet. "We don't have much time."

"We could let it go," Ivanko said. "This girl is bad news for us. Every time we get close to her it goes to shit. Just ask Sergei."

"I've no time to talk to a fucking corpse. She can identify Sergei, even if he is dead, and in turn, he will be linked to us. She must be eliminated. When the cop is on bereavement leave, the case will be transferred to Jenkins, and we will all be safe," Dimitri reminded him. "Or do you wish to question my leadership further?"

Ivanko backed down, thoroughly chastened. "No. I will follow whatever you command me to do."

Dimitri nodded. "Find the bitch and kill her. Leave the Irishman to me."

By the time Matt reached the scene, first responders were already there. Margaret's Volvo was wrapped around a streetlight, and Grant was sitting on the sidewalk while EMTs taped a cut above his eye. In all, it could have been, and he'd honestly expected it to be much worse.

Taking a deep breath, Matt climbed out of his car and walked over to where Grant was getting first aid. He pointed to the nasty gash over his eyebrow. "How'd that happen?" Matt asked. The airbags in the car had deployed, so there shouldn't have been any way of him busting his head open.

"Fucker hit me with the butt of his gun," Grant said with a grimace.

"Kaitlyn will kill me for getting your pretty face messed up," Matt said, unable to express his relief at seeing his best friend of nearly three decades reasonably unharmed. "Why didn't you call me back?"

"They took my damn phone," Grant said.

On his own phone, Matt pulled up the app to locate lost phones and plugged in the number. According to the map, the phone was only yards away from them. He called it and then followed the ringtone. It had been tossed carelessly into the bushes near the back door of Loralei's home.

Matt stooped to pick up the phone. As he closed his hand over it, he realized why they'd taken it to begin with. It was impossible to track a phone without the number, and having accessed Grant's, they had all the information they needed to be able to track Loralei. Fear exploded inside him.

"I'm taking one of the cruisers," he said to one of the uniformed officers, tossing the phone to him. "Get him home safe!"

Matt climbed behind the wheel of the cruiser and hit the lights, even as he was speed-dialing Loralei's number. He had a sick feeling in his gut. Shit was about to get real.

Seven

Ciaran awoke, the small cabin silent save for the even sounds of Loralei breathing next to him. It was wrong. There was such a thing as too quiet.

Outside, there was no sound. No birds called, no branches rustled. Everything was still.

On the nightstand, his phone blinked at him, the little green light alerting him to a message. Carefully and silently, he retrieved the device and scanned the text.

It was a warning from Matt, but it had come too late. Whoever was coming for them was already there.

Still lying back against the pillows, not wanting to be up, moving around, and making himself an even bigger target, Ciaran spoke softly.

"Loralei, it's time to wake up," he uttered.

"No," she mumbled in response and snuggled deeper into the pillows.

"I don't think you have a choice, love. They're here," he warned.

Her eyes opened, suddenly alert and wide awake. "How do you know? Did you hear something?"

"No. That's the problem. The whole house is quiet... power has been cut. Truck is probably disabled. I would have done that first if it were me," he replied, still keeping his tone barely above a whisper.

"What do we do?" she asked.

He hated to see her fear, hated to see the uncertainty in her eyes as she pondered their uncertain fate. It would be the last time, he swore, that she would have to feel that way.

Ciaran reached over the edge of the bed. The first article of clothing he found was her sweater, followed by his pants. He hauled them both up. "Put that on, but no large movements...move slowly, deliberately. Try to make as little noise as possible," he whispered.

"Do you think they can see us?" she asked.

"I don't know...but I wouldn't bet against it."

While Loralei donned her sweater, he slipped into his discarded jeans. Denim was hardly body armor, but he found himself reluctant to face off in a fight to the death with his dick hanging out.

There was no doubt for him that it would be a fight to the death. These weren't the kind of people who understood mercy on either end of it. Leaving them alive was inviting them to come back.

He'd stashed his guns just beneath the bed while Loralei had slept. Now, closing his hand around the hilt of one, he checked the clip and then flipped the safety to the off position. All the while, he listened. There was a slight scuffling sound on the porch, something that, had he been asleep, he might never have heard.

"When I tell you," he whispered, "I want you to hit

the floor and crawl to that fucking kitchen. The island is the only cover we have."

"Do you really think they're not going to just shoot through these walls?"

"These walls are twelve-inch-thick logs. They'll stop a bullet or, at the very least, make it ineffective. So just concentrate on getting to the kitchen where there's no direct path from any window in here."

"What about you?" she asked, her eyes wide with fear, tears shining in their depths.

"I'm going to end this in a less-than-law-abiding manner. Somehow, I don't think your brother will mind," he said as he grabbed one of the other guns he had at the ready. He pressed it into her hand.

"Ciaran, I don't want to lose you now," she said, even as she automatically checked the clip and flipped the safety off before looking up at him again. "If you screw up again, I want to have a chance to kill you myself."

He would have laughed. By God, he wanted to. "You'll get your shot, *mavourneen*," he vowed.

"I'm counting on it," she said evenly.

He held up three fingers and began to count off. By the time he hit two, a tiny green dot from a laser site was dancing around the room, trying to find a target.

At one, Loralei did as he'd asked. She crawled toward the kitchen even as the first shot shattered the glass at the back half of the cabin. Ciaran moved quickly, getting into position against that wall, ready and waiting for whoever came through that window first.

When the first volley of gunfire ended, the bed was shredded. Bits of fabric and the innards of the mattress flitted about the room like a macabre snowfall.

What came next left him reeling. It wasn't a person

who came through the window. Instead, they tossed in a small green canister.

"Fuck," he whispered and immediately turned his head away while covering his ears.

Even with his eyes squeezed tightly shut and his fists muffling the sound, the stun grenade was brutally effective at leaving his senses utterly worthless. All but blind and deaf from the concussive force and the flash, his stomach was rolling from the accompanying dizziness. Since he couldn't see shit in front of him, the gun was all but useless.

Somehow, he got to his feet, but he was still staggering when the first man came through the remnants of the broken-out window. The first blow landed, the punch sending him back against the wall. Immediately, he dropped to a crouch and his fist shot out, landing a crippling blow to the other man's balls. It was a cheap shot, but effective, and he couldn't afford to fight fair. They weren't.

"*Xyocec!*" the man cursed as he lifted his weapon to fire.

Ciaran never gave him the chance. With his limited vision, the only shot he had was to stay in close contact with the other man and fight by feel.

They grappled for control of the gun, of each other. Ultimately, Ciaran managed to get the assailant in a hold he couldn't break. Snapping someone's neck wasn't the simple thing it appeared to be in movies. Muscles tensed and resisted. The fight for survival and the adrenaline it produced had left them more evenly matched than he liked. Ciaran had the skill, but the other man was stronger, bigger.

Using his legs for more leverage, he tightened his hold around the man's neck and applied more force with his opposite hand. With continued pressure and an unrelenting need to protect Loralei and get them both out alive, Ciaran didn't stop until he heard that unmistakable sound. Whether the man was dead or alive, he wouldn't be a problem anymore.

Working to get to his feet again, he paused, still on his knees, when he felt the barrel against his temple. The flash of the grenade had decimated his peripheral vision and left him open. The second Russian had slipped in while they fought. Ciaran realized then that it had been the man's intent all along. The other one had been sacrificed like a pawn.

"You are smarter than I gave you credit for, Irish."

"Not bloody smart enough," Ciaran snapped.

The Russian shrugged. "It cannot be helped. You are like the Americans say...a Boy Scout. You play by the rules. And men like me, we make the rules. We always win."

"How the fuck would you know?" Ciaran shot back. "You never shut up long enough to find out!"

The Russian laughed. "It is a shame to put a bullet in your head. You have a way with words."

Ciaran didn't ask him not to. It was clear to both of them that the plan was already locked. "Just fucking get on with it then."

Loralei felt as if she were underwater. The sounds were muffled. She could barely make out the words through the ringing in her ears, and even when she could, they hardly made sense. Her stomach churned, and the urge to throw up was insistent.

Somehow, with some strength of will she hadn't

known she possessed, she managed to get to her feet. Her eyes burned as she tried to take in the scene before her. The flash of light had been so intense that even know, minutes later, she was still seeing spots and halos.

Only a few feet from her, she could see two figures. There was no discerning who was who for her. Her vision was too distorted to tell them apart, except for one thing.

"High or low?" she demanded.

The Russian's voice carried, the deep tones penetrating the fog left by the grenade. "You've been very difficult to track down, little shop girl."

"Ciaran," she said. "High or low?"

"High," Ciaran finally answered.

Loralei balanced her hands on the counter and squeezed the trigger. The first shot went wide. She knew it instantly. Shifting slightly and planting her feet for stability, she fired again. The dim figure of the man who had been standing jerked backward, and a word that was clearly a curse, even if she didn't understand it, escaped him.

Within seconds, she heard another shot, this time fired by someone else. It didn't take a lot of imagination to assume that Ciaran had finished him off. She wasn't sorry either.

Loralei sank to the floor and immediately threw up. The dizziness, the unimaginable pain in her head from the flash and concussion of the grenade, was just too much. Added to the fact that she'd just shot a man, and the man she was hopelessly in love with had just killed two men, vomiting and crying seemed like a perfectly legitimate response.

In the distance, the wail of sirens cut through the ringing. "Matt," she whispered.

"He's coming," Ciaran answered. "And you won't have to hide anymore."

She didn't answer, just closed her eyes, pressed her face against the cool wooden boards of the floor, and prayed for the waves of nausea to pass.

Eight

L oralei eased the tiny hybrid car to a stop in front of the house that was slowly starting to come together again. Ciaran had protested their assistance, but Matt and Grant had insisted. The roof had been patched, the siding replaced, now they were working on rebuilding the porch railings that had been shredded by gunfire.

Had it really only been a week? So much had happened during that time. She'd barely seen Matt until the day before, when he'd shown up on her doorstep exhausted and haggard. But he'd arrived with good news. They'd recovered enough pieces of the grenade canister to trace it back to Jenkins, cementing his ties to the Russians. He was going away for a long time.

She and Ciaran were back on track as well. It would never be smooth sailing for them entirely. They were both too proud and, she admitted it readily, a little too damaged for that. But she loved him enough to fight for him, and heaven knew he'd proved the same. There was only one tiny piece of the happy ending that still needed work. His family. Once again, she'd taken matters into her own hands.

"I don't know about this."

The words spoken from the passenger side of the car didn't quite penetrate. Loralei had been told there would be no permanent hearing loss from the grenade, but that it could take some time for her hearing to return completely to normal. Turning toward the passenger seat, she took in Mia Darcy's pale face and put two and two together.

"It will be fine," Loralei promised.

She was lying through her teeth. Ciaran had proven resistant on the subject of meeting his family, so she'd taken the initiative. She'd driven the short distance to Fontaine, cornered Mia in her office and blurted out, without tact or forethought, *hey, you have a half brother*.

In retrospect, she thought, it probably hadn't been the best of plans.

"What if he doesn't want anything to do with me?" Mia asked. "Let's face it...we are finding new and twisted ways to be more dysfunctional every day!"

Loralei turned her gaze back to the house. "He's very proud. And when he went to your father, and your father turned him away, it left him with certain ideas about the lot of you. Unfairly, I might add. But he didn't move halfway across the world to try and connect with his family on a whim. It's important to him, even if he won't admit how much just yet."

"I'm nervous," Mia admitted.

"You're shacking up with a man your father hates. The entire county is talking about you and this tragic, modern-day, star-crossed lovers bit...and you're worried about meeting a half brother?"

Mia rolled her eyes. "When you put it like that..."

Loralei grasped the door handle to get out of the car and made another promise she wasn't sure she'd be able to keep. "Come on. I'll introduce you. It will be fine."

Ciaran was carting away another load of shredded drywall. It was an unending task. Somehow, those fuckers hadn't left a wall in the place untouched. Between plumbing, electrical, and structural repairs, he wasn't sure that it wouldn't have been cheaper to just build a new house.

He reached the living room, now bare of any furniture as it too had been destroyed in a hail of bullets and stopped in his tracks. Loralei had let herself in with the key he'd given her. It was a symbolic gesture, as there had been holes in the wall he could have driven a truck through at the time.

It was the woman who entered behind Loralei that had him tongue-tied. It was the first time he'd been face-to-face with his half sister. Unexpected, terrifying, and more than a little infuriating, he turned to Loralei and threw his hands up in the air. The universal symbol for "what the fuck" only prompted a shrug from her.

"I thought," she finally replied, "that it was time you met your sister. Mia Darcy meet Ciaran Darcy, your half brother and generally the most sullen man I've ever met."

He said nothing at Loralei's less than gracious introduction, but instead watched the slow smile spread over the other woman's face. It was beautiful and welcoming. It terrified him.

"You must take after Quentin," she said softly. "He's the middle child, and he acts it in every regard."

"I don't know much about him," he replied cagily. He

was trying not to be rude because if he was, Loralei would make him pay for it. Also, in spite of how off-kilter he felt and how blindsided by her drop-in visit, he was actually incredibly pleased to see someone who shared his DNA and didn't hate him on sight.

"You wouldn't...mostly because our father is a gigantic, raging asshole. We don't have much to do with him. Ever. At all, if it can be avoided, honestly. He's sort of like a contagion," Mia answered.

"You're babbling," Loralei pointed out.

"I do that when I'm nervous," she snapped back.

"According to her, I do it all the time," Ciaran replied. "But, that and being Irish go hand in hand a bit. We like to talk."

Mia nodded. "Right...I know you haven't been here that long, and this is probably new for you, but I'd really like it if you came to Thanksgiving dinner."

Ciaran blinked at her. "I think that might be pushing it a little."

"No," she answered. "Thanksgiving dinner this year is going to be strange and all kinds of awkward. It'll be the Darcys and the Hayeses all under one roof... Because I'm apparently completely insane. We'll need you there. They outnumber us."

Ciaran considered it for a moment. "Do your older brothers know about this invitation?"

She blushed. "They don't actually even know about you yet."

"It's a bad idea," he said again. "Talk to them, and if you still want me to be there, I will...but only if all three of you are in agreement. I'll not be thrown out on my arse again."

Mia nodded. "I will. In fact, I'm going to go out to the car now and call them so I can meet with both of them tonight...and I'll just do that now so you and Loralei can fight about whatever it is you look ready to fight about."

The door closed softly behind her, and Ciaran found himself looking at the woman who had turned his life and his house upside down. "You can't ever leave well enough alone, can you?"

"Was it?"

"Was it what?" he asked sharply.

"Well enough," she replied as if he were an idiot.

He couldn't bring himself to lie and say yes. Instead, he just moved toward her and pulled her into his arms. He kissed her with a wicked intent, pressing her back against the door until they were chest to chest and hip to hip. When he broke the kiss, drawing back from her slowly and reluctantly, he said, "Sometimes, Loralei, a man likes to make his own decisions."

"And sometimes, when an intelligent and capable woman loves a man who is behaving like an idiot, she has to save him from his own decisions," she retorted. The reply lost some of its heat since she was breathless from the kiss.

"Is that why you did it? Because you love me?" he demanded.

"That's why I do pretty much everything," she admitted. "I know I meddled. I know I went behind your back... but if I hadn't, you'd be spending Thanksgiving alone, or God help us both, at my mother's house."

He shuddered at the thought. Anything was better than facing off against her ice queen of a mother. "And now I'll be spending it with total strangers who have no idea what the hell to make of me."

She laughed at that. "Trust me, you will be the least interesting thing happening at Thanksgiving. The Hayes and Darcy families have been feuding for more than forty years, and now they're all going to sit down at a table where someone gets to use a big knife? Yeah, they need you there just for security!"

"I'll go," he said, "on one condition."

"Oh?"

Ciaran smiled down at her. "You have to go with me. You'll sit right there beside me instead of under the scrutiny of your dragon of a mother."

"That's a done deal," she agreed. "I was already planning on it."

Ciaran's smile shifted into a grin. "It seems to me, I owe you a debt of gratitude...and I do like to pay my debts."

Her eyebrows shot up, and a smile that was pure flirtation curved her pretty lips. "What did you have in mind?"

"Take my sister back home, then you're going back to your house, you'll climb into that big bed of yours, wearing not a stitch..."

"And?" she prompted.

He kissed her again, hard and quick, before whispering against her ear, "I'll show you exactly why they call the Irish silver-tongued devils."

"You are so bad," she whispered.

"Only when you want me to be, love. Only when you want me to be."

Ciaran closed his arms around her for a moment, kissed her, and then stepped back. "I do owe you a debt of gratitude," he said seriously. "For giving me another chance when I don't bloody deserve it. But I promise you this, I'll spend my days trying to earn it...and every one of my nights."

She smiled at him, watery and overly emotional as she was wont to be. Loralei would forever have her heart on her sleeve, and he would do whatever it took to protect her from anything that might hurt her.

"I do love you," she whispered softly as she headed out the door to take Mia home.

"Aye. But I love you more," he said and meant every word of it.

A Look At Book Two

CLAYTON

He lost her once. He won't lose her again.

Clayton Darcy swore he'd never be like his father. But when the man threatened to destroy everything—his family, his business, his mother—Clayton fought back. He played dirty. And he won.

But victory came at a cost.

Six months ago, Annalee gave him a choice—be honest or walk away. He let her go, convinced it was the only way to protect her. Now, the war is almost over, and there's only one thing left to fight for. Her.

But Annalee isn't the woman he left behind. She's stronger now. Colder. And she's not about to let Clayton waltz back into her life just because he suddenly decides he wants her again.

Too bad Clayton has never been one to accept defeat.

As past betrayals resurface and old enemies close in, the battle for redemption turns deadly. Because in their world, love isn't a fairytale—it's a war. And Clayton intends to win.

AVAILABLE JUNE 2025

Chasity Bowlin is a *USA Today* bestselling author of numerous romance novels. She resides in central Kentucky with her husband, their charming son, and a lively menagerie of animals. A passionate traveler, Chasity enjoys weaving glimpses of her real-life adventures into her stories. As an avid Anglophile, she adores all things British, with a particular love for the Regency era.

Born and raised in Tennessee, Chasity spent much of her childhood with her doting grandparents, where soap operas and back-to-back episodes of Scooby-Doo were part of her daily routine. Her path to becoming a romance novelist was perhaps inevitable—her Barbie dolls didn't just cruise in pink convertibles; they traveled through time, hosted extravagant dinner parties, and one even had an evil twin locked in the attic.

www.chasitybowlin.com

www.ingramcontent.com/pod-product-compliance
Lightning Source LLC
Chambersburg PA
CBHW011457170626
46814CB00009B/3088